ETOBICOKE

PUBLIC LIBRARIES

MISSING ELMBROOK PARK

ETOBICOKE
PUBLIC LIBRARIES
CRANBROOK PARK

ALSO BY T.G. GILPIN

Death of a Fantasy Life (Quartet 1988)
Is There Anybody There? (Constable 1991)

Missing Daisy

T.G. Gilpin

This edition published in Great Britain in 1998 by
Allison & Busby Ltd
114 New Cavendish Street
London W1M 7FD

First published by
Constable & Co Ltd in 1995

Copyright © T.G. Gilpin 1995

The right of T.G. Gilpin to be identified as author of this
work has been asserted by him in accordance with the
Copyright Designs and Patents Act 1988.

This book is sold subject to the condition that it shall not, by way of trade
or otherwise, be lent, resold, hired out or otherwise circulated without the
publisher's prior written consent in any form of binding or cover other than
that in which it is published and without a similar condition including this
condition being imposed upon the subsequent purchaser.

A catalogue record for this book is available from the
British Library

ISBN 0 74900 326 X

Printed and bound in Great Britain by
Mackays of Chatham Plc
Chatham, Kent

For Joan and Barney

THE AUTHOR

T.G. Gilpin was born in Southampton in 1946. He has spent most of the last two decades teaching English as a foreign language in Spain, Zambia and Saudia Arabia. After six years in Singapore as senior lecturer at a polytechnic and as a tutor in phonetics at Singapore University, he returned to England in 1985. He is married with one daughter and now lives in Bristol.

1

'It's not a divorce,' his mother said. 'It's a trial separation. Do you know what that is?'

Alex knew what it was. It was a divorce.

'We both want to be on our own for a while. To see how we get on. Your father's going to live on his own for a bit.'

He knew she was lying to him. He could hear it in her voice. And he recognized the signs – like telling him what things weren't before she told him what they were, like pretending that the problem was going to be his own failure to understand.

Alex had come in from school and gone upstairs to take his uniform off and put his homework books in his room and then he had come down and asked her what time his father was coming home. Sometimes he came home in time for dinner and sometimes he didn't get in from work until after Alex's bedtime. When he didn't come home for dinner, there was a big row after Alex had gone to bed and his mother was in a horrible mood all the next day.

She had ignored his question and asked him how he'd got on at school. Then she'd gone into the kitchen and she was in there a long time fiddling about before she had called him through and told him.

She was standing in the kitchen holding a cup which she had started drying, twisting the cloth between her fingers. He noticed that she'd varnished her nails. She looked beautiful, but then she always looked beautiful.

'He just needs to be on his own,' she said. 'He isn't going to live with somebody else, if that's what you think.'

There it was again. Had Alex said that this was what he thought? So why mention it? Besides, he knew this was a lie. He wasn't deaf, his mother was hopeless at keeping her voice down, and he hadn't been at secondary school for a year without knowing what 'slag' meant.

'It's a temporary arrangement,' she said. 'For the time being. Just to see how we get on.'

This was stupid. Alex sometimes thought that adults were all stupid. They try to make things out to be complicated when they're really simple. Parents are either married or they're not. They either live together or they don't. They either love each other or they don't. There were boys at school whose parents were divorced and lived apart. His parents were not like that. They were married, they lived together and they loved each other. Or that was how it was supposed to be. If this was wrong, then it was completely wrong. There was no in-between. There was nothing in the middle.

'When's he going?' he said.

'He's gone. He went this morning.'

Alex just stood and looked at her. He couldn't believe it. They'd actually done it. They'd waited until he was out of the house, they'd waited until he was at school and then they'd done it behind his back.

'We were going to tell you last night,' she said. 'Then we thought . . . well, we thought it was better not to.' She finished drying the cup and hung it on a hook.

He'd known they'd been up to something last night. They'd talked downstairs for ages after he'd gone to bed, but quietly. They weren't having a row.

'When's he coming home?'

'Don't be silly, Alex,' she said. 'I've just told you. He's gone to live on his own.'

Of course he should have seen it coming. They must have been plotting it for months. He'd known most of

6

what was going on, but he'd never imagined they'd go this far. He didn't think it could happen to him.

She dried another cup and hung it up and put the cloth over the back of a chair.

'Where's he living?'

She didn't answer the question.

'Give me a cuddle,' she said, 'there's a good boy.'

He put his arms round her and she kissed him on the cheek. She hadn't done that for a long time. Then she knelt in front of him and held his face between her hands. He could smell the new nail varnish.

'We're going to have to be very nice to each other, Alex.'

She kissed him again and stood up.

'It won't be very different, really,' she said. 'You can see him at weekends. Go to the pictures. Maybe a few evenings after school. We'll just be on our own a bit more. Just you and me. You won't mind that?'

'No,' he said.

Alex knew the danger he was in but he couldn't say anything. Somebody at school would find out. They were bound to. Somebody always found out. He couldn't tell her about school. He couldn't tell her what it was like. It wasn't as bad now as it had been in his first year, but it was bad enough. There were people who made it their business to make his life a misery. Now they would have something else to use against him. His father had left home and gone to live with a slag. They would never let him forget it, never, not for a minute of the day, not for the rest of his life.

The story about seeing his father at weekends didn't even last the evening. Later on, when he was upstairs doing his homework, he heard her on the phone to one of her friends. He opened his door very quietly and crept out to the top of the stairs.

'If he wants to live with her,' she was saying, 'let him. Let him pay for it. House. Contents. Car. Maintenance. No

7

access to the boy while he's with her. If he tries to come near the boy, I'll see the bastard in court.'

'Norman,' somebody said quietly, and then a little louder, 'Noorrman.'

They were waiting for the last lesson of the afternoon. Outside the classroom windows, the sky was clear blue. Tonight would be frosty. Next week, after the clocks had gone back, it would be getting dark by this time. The first cars were beginning to pull out of the car-park. Some of the teachers were getting away early.

'Noorrman.'

Form 2B, who had had a hard day, were looking forward to a little light relief. They had English with Norman Farrow. Norman was a new teacher and they could do what they liked with him.

The chorus was picked up around the classroom.

'Noorrman. Nooorrrman.'

The voices grew louder and the first syllable of Norman's name grew longer and longer. The trick was to say it just loud enough so that he might have heard it as he came down the corridor, but not so loud that he could make a definite accusation. Alex did not take part in this. It was his first day at school since his father had left home. He had spoken to no one all day and had avoided anyone who might speak to him. He had other things on his mind.

'Nooorr –' Suddenly there were footsteps outside and the classroom door opened, but the face which appeared round the door was not that of Norman Farrow. It was the dreaded Potter.

Mr Potter stood in the doorway and glared at them until there was absolute silence, then he continued to stand there and glare at them. He was a short man but stocky and strong, with thinning hair and a bushy beard. It was

8

well known in the school that you did not mess about with George Potter. There was just something about him. Some teachers had it and some didn't.

When he was finally satisfied that he had their attention, he spoke.

'Is this 2B?'

'Yes, sir.'

Mr Potter seemed to take a very long time to decide whether this was an acceptable answer. There was silence in the room.

'And what precisely,' he said, 'was that noise which greeted me as I came down the corridor?'

There was no answer. They all just stared at him.

'It sounded like a herd of camels, in rut.'

No answer.

'Do you know what rut is?' he said to a boy in the front row.

'No, sir.'

'Good.' He glared round the room again. 'Now,' he said, '2B, I have been asked to inform you that Mr Farrow will be ten minutes late. Ten minutes. While you are waiting, you will continue with the work you were doing in the last lesson. Is that clear?'

Nobody knew what they'd been doing in the last lesson, but they all said it was clear.

'And you will do it in silence.'

They fetched books out of their desks, opened them and stared at them, fiddling with their pens. A girl who was sitting next to Alex asked him what they were supposed to be doing. Alex shook his head and remained slumped in his chair, gazing at some private vision through the classroom window. She asked him again, leaning towards him across the gap between the desks and poking him with her finger. Alex shook his head again and pushed her away.

9

'You!' said Mr Potter in a booming voice. Everyone turned and looked round. It was a while before Alex realized that he was the one being looked at. 'Yes, you. Back row. Stand up.'

Alex pushed back his chair and stood up slowly. Somebody giggled. Mr Potter glared round the room and the giggling stopped.

'Stand up straight.'

Alex stood up straight, his eyes fixed on Mr Potter.

'Name?'

'Pelham.' It came out almost inaudible.

'What?'

'Pelham, sir.'

'Pelham, is it?' said Mr Potter, as if a great mystery had just been solved.

'Yes, sir.' Alex knew that he was red in the face and he could feel the hairs prickle on the back of his neck. He knew everybody was looking at him. They seemed to be staring straight in front of them, but he knew they were really all looking at him.

Mr Potter walked slowly over to the window and stood looking out, his hands clasped behind his back.

'Well, Pelham,' he said, 'since you do not seem to know how to sit on a chair, you will remain standing until a teacher tells you to sit down.' He turned round. 'Is that clear?'

'Yes, sir.' More giggles.

Mr Potter glared at them again and there was silence. When he was satisfied that everything was in order and that his instructions were being carried out, he turned his back on them and walked out of the room.

Alex stood, waiting for Norman, or someone, to come and tell him to sit down. People kept turning their heads and grinning at him. Midgeley, who was one of his principal tormentors, had turned right round in his chair and was pulling faces at him.

This was just the worst thing that had ever happened to him. This was worse than having both your arms and legs blasted off by a shotgun in a bank raid. Worse than having your head explode. Worse than being captured by the living dead who cut you open and eat up your insides while you're still alive. Alex had experienced all these things, but this was the worst yet.

He decided that he hated George Potter more than anybody else in the whole world.

2

It was Saturday morning, a week before the birthday party. Daisy was sitting at the table dunking a soldier through the roof of her boiled egg. Sarah had finished her own breakfast before Daisy got up. This gave her time for the ritual of finding out what Daisy wanted for breakfast. On schooldays they did a short form of it but at weekends it tended to go on a bit.

Daisy was a fussy child where her food was concerned. She always had been. Even as a baby, when all she ate was flavoured goo out of pots from the chemist's, she had had very particular likes and dislikes. Things had to be exactly right. At one time Sarah had been paying an extra thirty pence a half-dozen for free-range eggs because Daisy wouldn't eat the ordinary ones. Then she discovered that Daisy could tell the difference between the boxes. She kept a free-range box and put ordinary eggs in it. Daisy ate the eggs.

Sarah couldn't remember when the breakfast ritual had started. She had to guess what Daisy wanted. The first few guesses had to be serious.

'Cornflakes?'

'No.'

'Bread and marmalade?'

'No.'

Then they started to get silly.

'A glass of water and a clip round the ear?'

'No!'

When Daisy got tired of this, she would reveal what she wanted. This morning, after a particularly lengthy version of the ritual, it had been a soft-boiled egg with soldiers, toasted soldiers.

'I want to see all those eaten up,' Sarah said. 'Every last one.'

'Every last one,' said Daisy.

She looked up at her mother and smiled. She wiggled the soldier out through the top of her egg, popped it in her mouth whole and then set about selecting another from the troop on her plate. Sarah stood and watched her.

In a week's time it would be six years since Daisy had come into the world, unwanted and unloved. Sarah was not married. Her relationship with Daisy's father had gone downhill from the moment they discovered she was pregnant. When Daisy was three months old, he had walked out of the house one day and she hadn't seen him since. Daisy had been an accident, a mistake. There had been times when Sarah had called her a horrible mistake, though never in front of Daisy – or, at least, not since she had been old enough to understand.

It was all different now. That part of her life seemed remote, unreal. Slowly, day by day, as Daisy had grown up, everything had changed. Daisy had given her life a shape, a pattern, a purpose. Daisy was the centre of her life now.

Today was an important day, almost as important as the birthday. Today was the fitting for Daisy's party dress. Sarah had been to the sales and bought a yard and a half of bright red material and Val Kellett was making it up into a dress for the party next Saturday. Val taught home economics at the secondary school where Sarah worked preparing school meals. It was convenient because it was just across the road from Daisy's primary. A lot of the teachers were sniffy about talking to the catering staff, but Val had always been friendly. Sarah had mentioned that she'd like Daisy to have a new dress for the party but she couldn't afford it, and Val had offered to make one up if Sarah bought the material. Val was good at anything like that, anything practical.

Daisy's fitting was at ten o'clock. After breakfast, Sarah let her watch television for half an hour while she washed up the breakfast things and did some cleaning. She had phoned Val the evening before and arranged to take Daisy to her house at ten and leave her there while she went to the local supermarket to do the weekend shop. She would collect her on the way home, by which time the dress would be ready except for a few finishing touches.

When it was nearly time to go, Daisy went into her room to get dressed and Sarah went with her to supervise. Left to herself, Daisy was capable of putting on some treasured garment full of patches and darns which would be revealed when she got undressed for the fitting. When Sarah had satisfied herself about Daisy's appearance, and sent her to the bathroom once more so that she wouldn't have to ask to go at Val's, they set off.

They left the house at a quarter to ten. It was a sunny morning after another frosty night, and Daisy skipped along the street holding Sarah's hand.

'Can we bring the dress home today?' she said.

'No, darling, it won't be ready. I'll pick it up in time for your birthday.' Actually, it might have been ready, but Sarah didn't want to bring it into the house in case Daisy tried it on and got it dirty before the party. Daisy had to look her best. She had invited all her friends from school and some of the younger children from the estate, and all the mothers would be there.

They reached the main road which marked the boundary of the estate and crossed at the traffic lights. As soon as they were on the pavement on the other side, Daisy started tugging at her mother's hand, trying to break free.

'I know the way from here.'

'Not just yet,' Sarah said, keeping a tight grip on Daisy's wrist. There was a lot of traffic even on the minor roads. She knew Daisy was really too old to be treated like this, but she was incapable of walking in a straight line. She was always skipping and jigging about, and Sarah still had nightmares about her running out into the road.

The area on this side of the main road was a lot nicer than the estate. The streets were wider and the houses were semis not terraces and they had proper gardens. Val had a big three-storey house which had belonged to her parents. It had a garden with fruit trees.

'Can I ring the bell?' Daisy said. The door bell at Val's had a chime which played a tune.

'Yes, but only once.'

When they reached the safety of the lanes, Daisy wriggled her hand free and set off at a run.

'Be careful,' Sarah said. 'You'll fall over.'

Daisy stopped, half turned to look back at her mother, smiled and ran on. Sarah let her go. There was no danger here – no roads to cross, nowhere she could get lost.

There were lanes like these all over this part of the town, running between the backs of the houses, linking the streets, cutting off corners, offering short-cuts. The lane Daisy was on ran straight ahead from where Sarah was standing and past the wall at the bottom of Val Kellett's garden. There was a gate in the wall but Val always kept it locked, so you had to go round to the front. Further on, the lane was just wide enough for a car to come in from the other end, but Daisy didn't have to go that far. When she reached the wall, she had to turn left into another lane which ran along beside the garden and brought her out into the street next to Val's front door.

Sarah started after her, then she thought how silly she'd been holding Daisy's hand all the way and how excited Daisy would be going up to the door and ringing the bell on her own. She would be out of Sarah's sight for no more than a minute before she reached the house.

'I'll pick you up in half an hour, darling,' she said. 'Do be careful.'

She watched Daisy turn the corner at the garden wall and then she began walking back towards the main road.

A little over half an hour later, Sarah was standing outside Val Kellett's door. She put her shopping bags down and rang the bell. Val opened the door, looked at her rather coldly and walked back into the house. Sarah picked up her shopping and followed her through into the living-room.

Val's next-door neighbour, Cathy Pelham, was there. Sarah had met her a couple of times before. She had a son, Alex, in the second year at the school. She was sitting in an arm-chair with a cup of coffee and a plate of biscuits in front of her. In the centre of the room was the headless, limbless torso of a tailor's dummy with Daisy's party dress draped over it. The dress didn't seem much further on than the last time Sarah had seen it. There was no sign of Daisy.

Val picked a cigarette up off the table and lit it.

'I like to be told,' she said, 'all right? For the next time? I do like to be told, OK?'

Sarah didn't know what she was talking about. She was looking round for Daisy.

'If you're going to be half an hour late,' Val said, 'it would be nice to be told.' She looked at Sarah. 'Where's

15

Daisy? Didn't you bring her? I thought I was supposed to be doing this bloody dress.'

It was Cathy Pelham who reacted first to the expression on Sarah's face.

'My God,' she said, 'what's wrong? You look awful.'

Sarah said nothing. She just stood in the middle of the room and stared at the headless dummy wearing Daisy's dress.

Sefton Road was a very respectable road. No doubt there were roads over on the estate where all kinds of peculiar behaviour were tolerated but Sefton Road was not like that. It was the sort of road where people politely acknowledged their neighbours but did not enquire into their business and saw no great need to know their names. It was the sort of road that took a dim view of some mad woman running up and down screaming and banging on doors.

Val and Cathy managed to get her back into the house. Sarah was hysterical. Val took charge.

'If she's lost,' she said, 'where would she –'

'Lost?' said Sarah. 'How can she be lost? I saw her go down the lane.'

'OK, something's happened. Maybe she rang the bell and I didn't hear her. She wandered off.'

'She wouldn't,' Sarah said. 'She wouldn't.'

'Phone the police,' Cathy said.

'OK, I'll phone the police.' Val was puffing on another cigarette and striding up and down the room. 'I'll stay here in case she comes back here. Cath, you've got the car? Take Sarah home in case she goes home. I'll get the police to go there as well. We should have people in both places in case she turns up.'

'She wouldn't,' Sarah said.

Cathy held Sarah by the shoulders and steered her out to the car. Val was on the phone as they went out of the door.

Cathy had noticed in the car that Sarah smelt. Was it sweat? She smelt as if she'd wetted herself.

Where were the bloody police? They'd been back at Sarah's house for half an hour. There was no sign of Daisy. Sarah was climbing the walls.

Cathy phoned the police. They said someone was on their way.

When they arrived, she started screaming at them. They said their response time was good. They said they'd received Miss Kellett's call only a few minutes before Cathy's. ('Lying bastards,' Val said when she was told.)

When Daisy could not be found, the police cordoned off the lanes and began combing every inch. It was in effect, if not yet in name, a murder investigation. They took away bags full of gravel, cigarette ends, waste paper, milk cartons, beer cans, dog muck. Everything was microscopically examined. There was nothing to suggest that Daisy had ever set foot in the lane. There was no sign of a struggle.

Somewhere between the bottom wall of Val Kellett's garden and the point at which the lane came out into the street, a distance of about forty yards, Daisy seemed to have vanished as cleanly as if she had been plucked up into the air and spirited away.

The people in the neighbouring houses had seen nothing out of the ordinary. People who had been walking along the road that morning had seen nothing. A van had been seen entering the lanes from the far end, but that was around eleven o'clock, an hour after Daisy's disappearance. The police were anxious to trace the driver. No one

17

had seen anything suspicious. No one had heard screams. No one had seen a little girl fighting for her life.

3

'Have you thought about that little girl?' his mother said. 'Have you thought what she must be going through?'

She'd been talking about the little girl for days. Apparently she'd had to cope with the mother until the police arrived.

Alex had been quite excited about the little girl at first. There had been police all over Sefton Road with police vans and dogs and everything. It was as good as a film. They'd questioned everybody in all the houses to find out if they'd seen anything. They'd questioned Alex. He'd considered giving them the crucial piece of information they needed to solve the case, but he couldn't think of anything appropriate on the spur of the moment and he thought it might be risky making up stories for the police. They tend to check that sort of thing.

'There are other people in the world besides you, you know.'

Alex didn't see what this had to do with it. If some little girl he didn't even know was worse off than she might have been, that didn't make him any better off.

'You should think of other people sometimes, Alex.'

All he had done was to ask her, again, where his father was living and why he couldn't go and see him.

'You're twelve now, Alex,' she said.

She was always saying this. You're eleven now, Alex. You're twelve now, Alex. You're nearly thirteen, Alex. Whatever age he was, it was exactly the age at which he shouldn't be saying what he was saying.

It was nearly his bedtime. He'd finished his home-work and had his bath and he was sitting in the living-room in his pyjamas. His mother had been in quite a good mood until now. They'd watched some television together and then she'd talked to him a lot about how well he was getting on at school and how pleased the teach-ers were with him. Val had said so. Miss Kellett lived next door and she was a teacher at the school. Everybody said how well he was doing. So, since she was being so nice to him and telling him what a good boy he was, he thought it was worth asking about his father. He'd been wrong.

'You could give me his phone number,' he said. 'Then I could talk to him. I wouldn't ask him where he was. I promise.'

'Don't keep on about it, Alex.'

'Just a phone number.'

'I haven't got his phone number.'

Alex was being clever here, putting her off her guard. The fact was that he'd been doing some detective work and he already knew the number. What he was after was the address, but that wasn't going to be easy. He had to start by just getting her to tell him something, anything.

He'd phoned the office where his father worked. They'd said he was out but they'd given a home number. When Alex phoned the number, a woman answered. The slag. He had slammed the phone down without speaking. He hadn't called back. He'd called Directory Enquiries and asked for the address that went with that number, but they wouldn't give it to him.

'I don't see it would do any harm,' he said. 'Just a num-ber.'

She'd started looking at a magazine, flicking through the pages, while she was talking to him. Suddenly, she put it down and looked up at him, quickly, fiercely. He knew that look. It was the way she looked at him when he'd done something wrong, something very wrong. Only this time, she didn't look angry. She looked frightened.

'Alex, are you lying to me?'

'No.'

'Alex. . . .'

'No,' he said. Oh God, how much did she know? How did she know? They'd phoned her back from the office and told her about his call. Or somebody had the phone tapped.

'Has he phoned you?'

'No.'

'Has he phoned you, Alex? You must tell me if he's phoned you. I'll know if you're lying.'

'No.'

'Has he tried to see you at school?'

'No,' he said. It was all right. She didn't know anything. She didn't know about the call. He was safe.

'Don't lie to me, Alex.' She was sitting forward in her chair, staring into his eyes with that terrible look on her face, as if this time he had done something really, really bad.

'I'm not. Honest.'

'Promise me, Alex.'

'I promise.'

She seemed to accept this. She closed her eyes and took a deep breath. She sat for a long time with her eyes closed. Alex waited for whatever was coming next. Then she got up from her chair and came over to where he was sitting. He almost flinched away from her. But she knelt on the floor in front of his chair and put her hands on his knees and looked up at him.

'I know this is hard for you to understand,' she said. 'You do want him to come back to us, don't you?'

'Yes.'

'Well, the only way he'll ever come back is if you trust me and do what I say. It doesn't matter if you don't understand now. You will one day. Just trust me. Don't ever lie to me, Alex.'

Alex shook his head. She looked down towards the floor and her fingers dug into his knees.

'I know it must seem as if we're being very hard on him,' she said. 'And hard on ourselves.' She was speaking very softly now. 'But it's for the best. You'll see.'

She looked up at him again and her voice was stronger.

'If he tries to get in touch with you, you must tell me. If he phones you. If he tries to see you at school.'

'Yes,' Alex said.

'You'll tell me?'

'Yes.'

'Solemn promise?'

'Yes.'

She stood up and put her arms round him and kissed him.

'You wouldn't do anything to hurt me, would you?'

'No,' he said, 'never.'

She kissed him again and ruffled his hair.

'Don't ever betray me, Alex,' she said. 'I don't think I could stand it.'

Things had been chaotic for a week. There had been lessons cancelled every day and kids were being taken out of class every five minutes. The police had been around in droves, talking to the whole school year by year and interviewing anybody who thought they might have seen something. The secondary was just across the road from the school the little girl had gone to, and they thought somebody might have been seen hanging around.

Still, chaos had something to be said for it. Norman had had two classes cancelled with 2B, for which relief much thanks. The whole staff had trouble with 2B, but Norman had more trouble with them than most.

21

The problem was that he was new, not only new to the school but new to teaching. It was his first job. Also, he was a teacher of English. English was not a matter of drilling facts. An enjoyment of English required a certain sensitivity, a certain receptiveness, a certain intellectual curiosity even. There were one or two of them who would probably have been all right in a different class, but in general the sensitivity quotient in 2B was not high.

It had been a few weeks before he realized that they were out of control. They were quite cunning about it. At first they had feigned an interest in what they were doing. The noise level, though excessive, had been consistent with a healthy enthusiasm for their work. He reprimanded them gently.

This was his big mistake. His correct procedure, he now realized, would have been to go completely ape and put a stop to it there and then. When he failed to do so, the noise had grown by carefully calculated increments to its present level. The trouble was that it was impossible to pick out individual culprits. They managed to achieve a general hubbub of unidentifiable voices which bordered on the deafening. It was only a matter of time before his colleagues started complaining.

The only person he had confided in about his problems was Val Kellett. There was no one else on the staff that he trusted. He had thought of talking to George Potter about it – the pupils regarded George with a sort of terrified awe of which Norman thoroughly disapproved and was madly envious – but he wasn't sure of his ground with George. Besides, talking to Val was a pleasure and Norman didn't have many pleasures.

He didn't know why he found her so sexy. She was probably ten years older than him, early thirties. She had no figure worth mentioning. She always wore trouser suits so he didn't know what her legs were like. She wasn't conventionally attractive at all. She was tall for a woman, slim and very pale with yellowy hair drawn back tight into a pony tail. The only really striking thing about her was the almost ghostly whiteness of her skin, her complete lack of colour.

She was just so easy to talk to, and Norman had never found talking to women easy. He had told her the whole problem.

'You ought to talk to somebody in the English department,' she said. 'Have a word with Derek about it.' Derek Hodge was his head of department.

'I'd rather not.'

'How about George? Tell him what you're doing, how you go about it. I'm sure he'd be sympathetic.'

'Spell?' said George in a loud voice. 'You're not teaching them to spell, are you? You'll have them punctuating next.' He knew Derek Hodge was in earshot. 'What are you trying to do, stifle their creativity?'

'I do correct it sometimes,' said Norman, 'when it gets too bad.'

Derek didn't rise to the bait, but George could hear the pages of his newspaper rustling.

'You're on thin ice there, my son,' said George. 'Very thin ice.'

'I don't think it does any harm from time to time,' Norman said.

'Spelling,' said George slowly, drawing out the syllables and wagging his head as if contemplating some abstruse notion on the fringes of educational theory, 'I'd be careful about that. Besides, people might start wondering where you learnt it.' He gave Norman a long, level stare. 'I hope you haven't been reading books again.'

There was more rustling of the newspaper. Derek got up and walked out of the staffroom.

George slapped Norman on the back. He wasn't being fair. Norman had only been out of training college for five minutes and he desperately wanted to please everybody.

This sort of thing wasn't nearly as much fun as it had been when Pris Hodge was head of English. It was a year since she'd been promoted to county adviser, bequeathing the department to her husband, and some of the sparkle had gone out of George's life.

'I wouldn't worry too much, Norm,' he said. 'They probably don't take any notice of you.'

'That's true,' said Norman.

Pris would have had a blazing row with him there and then. Derek just slunk away and reported George's latest outrage back to wifey when he got home in the evening. There was nothing Pris could do but fume quietly and plot revenge. It wasn't as much fun as pistols at dawn across the staffroom.

'I'm not against error correction in principle,' said Norman, with uncharacteristic bravado. 'It's just, well, it must be a bit boring from their point of view.'

'Now listen to me,' George said, putting his arm round Norman's shoulder, 'and I mean this seriously. The one thing you must never ever do in your teaching career is to see it from their point of view. One glimpse of their point of view and you're a marked man.'

'I don't know about that, George.'

'Your job is to knock an education into them, right? Their job is to resist. That's how it is. If you start seeing it from their point of view, they'll eat you alive. It's not a good idea to see things from the enemy's point of view while he's shooting at you. You might forget to shoot back.'

'I don't know if I see them as the enemy, exactly.'

'Pity,' George said. 'That's how they see you.'

The bell rang. People slowly folded up their newspapers and finished their coffee. They began to move a bit faster when Don Prewitt put his head round the door. He glanced round the staffroom and spotted George.

'Mr Potter,' he said, 'just the man. Are you teaching this period? Sorry to interrupt, Mr Farrow.'

The headmaster always used surnames outside the confines of his office in case there were any pupils about who might be led into impropriety by the discovery that teachers had first names.

'No, Don, not this period,' George said.

'Could I have a word?'

'Certainly, Don.'

'My office, then, Mr Potter?'

George nodded. The headmaster backed out into the corridor, holding the door open for two of the women who were on their way to class. Norman wearily picked up his pile of exercise books from the table.

'I just don't know when to take you seriously, George,' he said as he set off for his next period of trench warfare.

'I know,' George said. 'I have the same problem.'

When he arrived in Don Prewitt's office, George found himself invited to tea and biscuits. This was ominous. The headmaster's Earl Grey and digestives were normally reserved for heads of department and the barons of lower, middle and upper school.

It turned out that Don did not have any particular topic of conversation in mind. It was a friendly chat. George was on his guard. He had known for some time that the Hodges were out to get him, and he suspected Prewitt of being on their side in the interests of a quiet life. Since her promotion to county adviser, Hodge *femme* was in a position of real power. With Derek installed as head of English and reporting on everything that went on at the school, she would have all the ammunition she needed. He would have to tread carefully.

Oh, why the hell should he? Provided he didn't do something really stupid like inaugurating a programme of hands-on sex education for the first form, they couldn't touch him.

His disagreement with the Hodges ran deep. George saw himself as a traditionalist. His job was to teach his pupils something which he knew and they didn't, namely the correct use of the English language. It was a plain fact that the only method by which they could be persuaded to accept such an education was the one employed to persuade the Russian peasantry to accept collectivization. He had always found in dealing with his pupils that abject terror was highly conducive to a happy learning situation.

The Hodges were not of this opinion. They were progressive. Far be it from them to suggest that they knew anything which their pupils did not. We were all chums together, developing our personalities and exploring our creativity in a harmonious environment. We did not sit around reading hard books with long words in.

In keeping with this philosophy, Derek was illiterate. George had at one time started a collection of Derekisms, which he had been dissuaded from offering to the staff newsletter. He carried a notebook with him which included entries such as 'D. H. referred to me as the egregious Potter. Silly sod thinks it means very nasty' and 'D. H. accused me of meretricious argument. What does this argument do with itself? Stand about on street corners in a tight skirt and fishnet stockings?'

These things were important. In George's opinion the country had gone into terminal decline when people started saying 'cheers' instead of 'thank you' and bunging an apostrophe into anything with an 's' at the end.

26

His suspicions were further aroused by the sight of Don Prewitt in his informal man-of-the-people mode. He had taken his jacket off. There was something incongruous about Prewitt without a jacket, like a priest in a collar and tie. It made you wonder what he was up to.

George usually got on quite well with the head-master. Don was a few years older but they had come into teaching at about the same time. They belonged to a genera-tion which assumed that teachers knew how to spell and had mastered such technicalities as the use of the semi-colon. Prewitt had two faults, in George's opinion. One, he was a pompous old buffer who couldn't get to the point of any conversation without beating all around the bush and, two, he let the Hodges walk all over him. Pris had simply bullied him. Derek had never been known to row with anyone to their face, but he was all the more dangerous for that.

'How long have you been in teaching now, George?' said Don.

'Twenty-nine years,' George said, 'man and boy.'

'What are you now? Fifty-one, is it?'

'That's right.'

'I suppose the divorce will be going through soon,' Don said. 'That must be very stressful for you. They say it's one of the worst things –'

'It went through two years ago,' George said.

'Did it really? It seems only the other day that you and . . .' (The eye movement towards the file on his desk was almost imperceptible) '. . . Audrey were round for dinner.'

'It's donkey's years.'

'Is it really? You know, we must get together. One lunch time. We could go to the pub.'

Pub? This was presumably in deference to George's ple-beian tastes. He tried to imagine Prewitt in a pub. 'And a tankard of your best ale, landlord.'

'That would be nice,' George said.

'We all need to wind down, you know. After the stresses of the day.'

'Quite right,' George said.

This was the second reference to stress in the space of five minutes. Something was afoot. If it was what he thought it was, they had a fight on their hands.

'Your dad's left home, Smelham,' said Midgeley. 'My dad says your dad's left home.'

It was the moment Alex had been dreading. He had his head inside his desk. He was sorting out books for his homework. He kept his head down and carried on with what he was doing, passing the books slowly from one hand to the other, giving himself time to think. It had been almost over. A few more minutes and another day would have been over.

Midgeley was waiting for an answer.

'What?' Alex still had his head inside his desk. He had been expecting it. He'd known it was coming. Sooner or later somebody had to find out. He'd thought he was prepared for it, but he wasn't.

'Your dad's left home, Smelham.'

It could have been worse. There were only the two of them in the room. The whole class could have been there.

'No, he hasn't.'

'Yes, he has. My dad says he has.'

Alex pulled his head out of his desk and looked at Midgeley.

'I can't talk about it,' he said.

Midgeley stepped forward and slammed the desk lid down. Alex just got his fingers out in time.

'You'd better.'

Yes, he'd better. He had to. He knew he had to. Midgeley was several inches shorter than him but, as he knew to his cost, several times stronger. He'd better.

He'd almost survived another day. A few more minutes and he would have been safe. They'd had Norman Farrow for English, the last lesson of the day. It had been a shambles as it always was with Norman. Alex could have told him what he was doing wrong. He could have told him how to get the whole class eating out of his hand, but Norman was a teacher and Alex was twelve years old and Norman wouldn't have listened.

When the bell went, Mr Farrow had left the room and they had given him a few seconds to get down the corridor and then everybody had started playing the 'Norman, Norman' game. Then they had packed up their things and gone and only Alex and Midgeley were left. Midgeley had been on his way out of the door when he had turned and made his accusation.

Alex took a deep breath. It was now or never.

'If I tell you,' he said, 'you've got to promise not to tell anybody. The police don't want anybody to know.'

Midgeley said nothing, but he screwed up his eyes and his mouth fell open. Alex hadn't expected him to say anything. He hadn't expected any promises, but he knew he'd gained the advantage. He'd knocked Midgeley off guard.

'He witnessed a robbery,' Alex said. 'An armed robbery on a bank.' He disappeared inside his desk for a moment and brought out some more books. 'It was on the telly.'

'Your dad?' said Midgeley.

'Yes.'

Midgeley had not been prepared for anything like this. He'd expected a denial and he had his next line of attack ready. He wasn't quick enough to cope with a change of direction. He carried on as if he'd heard what he expected to hear.

'Your dad's left home, yes he has, because this man who works with my dad knows your dad and he says your

29

dad's moved into a flat next door to him. Your dad's in a flat in Gatehouse Road. That's what he told my dad.' Midgeley paused to allow the full weight of this evidence to sink in. 'Your dad's left home, Smelham.'

Midgeley had just earned Alex's undying gratitude, though he would never know why. All Alex wanted now was to get out of the room and walk home slowly and think about what he'd just learnt, think about what he could do with it. But he still had to deal with Midgeley. He'd begun his story and he had to finish it. He gripped the sides of his desk and put on a very serious face.

'He saw the robbers. He was outside the bank and he saw them before they went in, before they put their masks on, so he can identify them. Thing is,' Alex said, 'they saw him too. They know who he is. So the police have got to protect him. They've put him in a safe house where they can protect him if the robbers come after him. He can't stay with Mum and me. It'd be too dangerous for us if they came after him.'

This was too much for Midgeley. There he was looking forward to a bit of innocent Smelham-baiting to round off the day, and now this. He was speechless.

'So you see,' Alex said, 'you must never tell anyone. Never ever. Well, not until they're caught.'

Midgeley was completely won over. He too put on a very serious face and nodded agreement. Then he suddenly remembered what was supposed to have been his clinching piece of evidence.

'He's got a woman in there. Your dad's got a woman in there. This man my dad knows saw her going in and out.'

Alex had been ready for this.

'Policewoman,' he said. 'She's his bodyguard.'

'Bodyguard?' said Midgeley. 'A woman?'

'It's less suspicious. You know, in case the robbers find the place and they see her. She's a martial arts expert.' This was the least likely bit of the story but Alex couldn't think of anything better.

Midgeley wouldn't have known whether it was likely or not. At the mention of martial arts, he had leapt into a kung-fu posture and was advancing towards Alex chopping imaginary bricks in half in mid-air. He was just demolishing the last brick with a mighty whack when Miss Kellett put her head round the door.

'What do you think you're doing, Alexander Pelham?' she said.

Alex hadn't been doing anything, but of course he was the one she asked. Valerie Kellett was a friend of his mother's and she was also their next-door neighbour. She always made him feel awkward when she saw him at school. He liked people to stay in their compartments. Neighbours were neighbours and teachers were teachers. Miss Kellett was both and she knew too much about him. And why did she always have to call him by his full name when she saw him at school? When she saw him at home she called him Alex.

'Well?'

'Nothing,' he said.

'Nothing?' said Miss Kellett in mock astonishment. 'Then you ought to be doing something.' Why do all teachers think this is an original joke? 'You ought to be on your way home. Out of here, the pair of you.'

Alex gathered up his homework books and he and Midgeley slunk out of the room.

'Don't you run down the corridor, Alexander Pelham.'

Alex had no intention of running down the corridor. He walked very slowly to let Midgeley get well ahead of him. By the time he got to the front gate of the school, Midgeley was turning the corner at the end of the street still chopping bricks. Alex went the other way and took the long route home. He had a lot to think about.

He could never have guessed how it would turn out. He had lain awake at night and tried to imagine how he would feel at this moment. He had imagined how good he would feel when he had finally told his story and he had been believed. Now that it had happened, it didn't seem important any more. What he had learnt from Midgeley was much more important. Gatehouse Road. He didn't know where Gatehouse Road was, but he could find out.

At first he'd thought of using the story about the disappearance of the little girl. It had been in the papers and on the television and it had happened almost next door. The snag was that he couldn't think of any way of bringing his father into it. The robbery story was better. Besides, he disliked mixing truth and lies. When he did, he got confused about details and people could catch him out. If the whole story was a lie, he could make up his own details and people believed him.

It always surprised him that they believed him. He always felt as if he must be red in the face and sweating and stuttering and giving himself away with every word, but obviously he wasn't. People believed him. He had the knack.

When he got back home to Sefton Road, the lanes were still cordoned off but there didn't seem to be any police about except for a van parked further down the street. He stood at the end of the lane for a few minutes and waited to see if anything was going to happen, then he went into the house. His mother was on the phone and she didn't even notice he was late.

4

From the moment she heard the news, Dora Beale never doubted that her granddaughter was dead. When a man like that got hold of a little girl, he did his business with her and then he killed her. That was if he didn't kill her first and then do his business. They couldn't stop themselves. All she wanted was to see him caught and look him in the eyes and make him know what he'd done.

The day after Daisy's disappearance, she had rung Sarah and told her she was coming.

'All right,' Sarah said. No emotion in the voice. Nothing. Cold like a machine. She'd always kept her feelings to herself.

Sarah went away from the phone and Dora could hear her talking to somebody, then she came back and said the police would provide a car.

'I'm going to our Sarah's,' Dora said to her husband. 'You'll be all right.'

He took no notice of this and started fussing about, packing himself a bag. She soon put a stop to that. He'd been off work with his legs.

'And you needn't think you're coming.'

'I can get more time off,' he said. 'I asked.'

'You're not coming. Not with your legs.'

'I wasn't planning to walk.'

'You're more use here,' she said.

This wasn't true. He was no use anywhere. But she wasn't having him round her neck. She'd have enough to do coping with Sarah.

She arranged for a neighbour to come in and see to his meals.

'He'll be no trouble,' she said. 'He doesn't eat much.'

Between the disappearance of a child and the discovery of the body there is a time of waiting, like the time between a declaration of war and the first outbreak of fighting. It is a busy time, but there is an unreality about the busyness. The police have an investigation to conduct but they don't know for sure what kind of investigation it is. The press have a story to tell but they don't know what the story is. The public who read the newspapers and watch the television are outraged but they don't know exactly what they are outraged about. Everyone knows that this is no more than a prelude. Everyone is waiting for the storm to break.

When Dora arrived at her daughter's, she had found things both better and worse than she had expected. Worse because she hadn't realized there would be so many reporters. There were groups of them standing about outside the house watching every car that went past, there were more of them sitting perched on the garden wall like a flock of starlings waiting for crumbs, and there were vans with aerials on the roof parked all up and down the street. She practically had to fight her way into the house.

The good news was that Sarah was calm and keeping busy, though it didn't take Dora long to decide that she was too calm and too busy. She was busy preparing the house for Daisy's return. She'd cleaned it from top to bottom. They talked about what they would do when Daisy came home.

'What if she's not back for her birthday?'

'She'll be back,' Dora said. 'I'm sure she'll be back.'

'Do you think she's getting the right sort of things to eat?'

'I'm sure she is.'

'Things she likes?'

'Yes.'

Dora knew only too well that this sort of talk would have to come to an end, but she had quickly decided to go along with it. It wouldn't do Sarah any harm provided it didn't go on for too long. If it gave her comfort, let her believe it. It was better than watching her going out of her head. Dora just prayed that the body was found soon. She'd known a woman once who'd lost a child and never seen the body. She'd carried on like this for the rest of her life.

'She hasn't even got a change of clothes,' Sarah said.

They had gone out and bought presents for Daisy's birthday. The reporters followed them. Sarah wrapped the presents and lined them up along the living-room floor under the window so that they would be the first things Daisy saw when she came back into the house. The reporters photographed her with the presents.

The birthday had come and gone. The next week had come and gone. The reporters began to lose interest and drift away. There was nothing new to report. The police and an army of volunteers were searching the town yard by yard in widening circles outwards from the lanes, but there was no sign of Daisy. She seemed to have vanished off the face of the earth.

Once the house was no longer surrounded by reporters, neighbours began coming by to see if Sarah needed help with the cooking and cleaning. Dora soon put them straight about that.

'Much obliged,' she said, 'but she's got a mother.'

'Well, if there's anything you need.'

'Much obliged.'

People Sarah hardly knew came to the door to offer their sympathy. When she started going out of the house again, strangers would come up to her in the street with tears in their eyes. She was brusque, perhaps rude. She didn't know what to say to them. Some people merely stared at her and pointed her out to others.

As long as Daisy's body was not found, as long as there was still the possibility that she would be found alive, the feelings of shock and outrage which her disappearance

35

had aroused had no focus, no precise object. There was an intolerable vacuum. It was Sarah who would fill it.

She had already made an unfavourable impression on television. She had answered all the questions, given Daisy's description and described the clothes she was wearing, and made appeals to the public for information. She had appealed to anyone who might know of Daisy's whereabouts to return her safe and well. Everyone had commented on how well she was taking it, how normal she was, how controlled. This was double-edged. It was admirable in a way, of course, but was it entirely natural? Should she not be more disturbed?

Dora had also appeared on television. She said what a beautiful child Daisy was, an angel, the most wonderful child anyone could ever wish for. Sarah could have said this too, but it seemed beside the point that Daisy was wonderful. Daisy was Daisy. By contrast with Dora, Sarah gave the impression of being unmoved, almost uncaring. They stuck a camera in her face and held it there, waiting for the tears. There were no tears. She stared coldly into the lens.

One day, one of the newspapers reported that the police were concerned that Daisy had been out on the streets alone at the time of her abduction and that the mother was to be questioned again. This was untrue. The police were entirely satisfied with Sarah's original statement. The next day, the same report appeared in some of the other papers. Dora tried to keep the papers away from Sarah but she was afraid she might have seen them.

There was another reason for keeping the papers away from her. None of the reports on Daisy made any attempt to hide the assumption that she was dead. They talked about the probable motive and personality of her killer. Dora knew that Sarah would have to come to terms with Daisy's death, but it was better that she did it in her own way and her own time.

There was a change in Sarah's behaviour. She went quiet for a couple of days. She stopped talking about Daisy coming home. She hardly talked at all. She stopped cleaning the house. She just stared out of the window. Dora talked twice as much to break the silence.

'They don't think she's coming back, do they?' she said suddenly. She had been standing at the window with her back to Dora.

'Who, dear?' Dora said.

'Them.' She nodded her head towards the street outside the house where a couple of reporters and a camera crew were still standing about. 'They don't think she'll come back.'

'Of course they do.'

Dora didn't like the sound of this. It was too sudden.

'No, they don't.' Sarah stood looking out of the window. 'They don't want her to come home.'

'We all do.'

'They don't,' she said. 'They'll feel cheated if she comes home.'

Nothing more was said about it until, one day, when there were more reporters than usual outside, she went out and screamed at them in the street.

'Why aren't you out looking for her? What are you doing here?'

They stared at her and shuffled about and said nothing.

'You want her dead,' she said. 'You're just waiting for her to be dead.' It was the first time she had mentioned death.

She went back into the house and straight upstairs and shut herself in the bedroom. She locked the door and wouldn't let Dora in.

The reporters left her alone for a few days after this. When they came back, there were as many of them as there had been at the beginning. Their attitude was different,

37

and the questions had changed. Sarah refused to speak to them but they had a lot of questions for Dora.

'How often did you get to see Daisy, Mrs Beale?'

'Whenever I wanted to,' Dora said.

'Once a month, once a year?'

'Whenever I wanted.'

'Where's the father?'

'He's got no part in it. He didn't want any part in it when she was a baby. He hasn't got any part in it now.'

'Was she often out on the streets alone?'

'She was never out alone,' Dora said. 'Never. You ought to be ashamed of yourself asking a question like that.'

'You weren't here,' said one of them. 'How do you know?'

'I know.'

'She was alone when she was taken.'

'That's different.'

'Did she know about not talking to strangers?'

'Of course she did.'

'What's the father's name?'

'That doesn't matter,' Dora said. 'That's no business of yours. The police have got his name.'

'Don't worry, love,' they said. 'We'll find him anyway.'

If Sarah came out of the house they shouted questions at her.

'Have you got a boyfriend, Miss Beale?' (Before, they had called her Sarah or Mum. 'Can we have a picture of Mum with the presents?')

'How do you get on with your mother, Miss Beale?'

'What did you do with Daisy when you were working?'

'How did Daisy get on with your boyfriends?'

Sarah said nothing. She pushed past them with her head down.

'You're not doing yourself any good, you know,' one of them said.

38

The story in the papers began to change. At first the reports had been straightforward and accurate. They printed Daisy's picture, gave the circumstances of her disappearance and carried police appeals for information from the public. Sarah was described as bearing up. Now Daisy's picture continued to appear but Sarah's picture appeared more often. A new element was emerging. Sarah was becoming the centre of the story.

One paper reported that at the time of her disappearance Daisy had been sent out on an errand alone. Apparently, this was not unusual. She was regularly allowed to roam the streets alone. The next issue suggested that Sarah had locked her out of the house while she entertained a boyfriend. Neighbours were found who came forward to say that they had long been concerned for Daisy's welfare. Questions were asked as to why the social services had not been alerted.

Other papers followed up on the story. The house was soon under siege from reporters and Sarah couldn't go out. Dora went out and swore at them and told them to go away. They surged towards her waving microphones in her face and she had to escape into the house.

'When did you last see your granddaughter, Mrs Beale?'

'Were you worried about her, Mrs Beale?'

Dora had never seen anything like it. They were like a pack of dogs. Some of them were women, all made-up and hard-faced. They tried to be as bad as the men.

One newspaper had looked up the statistics and discovered that the abduction of a child by a stranger was a very rare crime. The culprit was usually a member of the family or someone known to the family, such as a boyfriend.

Daisy's father was located in Germany, where he had been living for the past three years with a wife and child. He appeared on television and spoke movingly of his grief.

He gave an account of the break-up of his relationship with Sarah from which she emerged in a worse light than before. The hunt for boyfriends was now on. Men she had been out to dinner with were interviewed about their association with her and invited to assess her as a sexual partner.

Under the headline DAISY – YOU VOTE, one newspaper conducted a poll and discovered that sixty-four per cent of its readers now believed that Sarah bore some responsibility for Daisy's disappearance. Forty-seven per cent thought that she knew more than she was telling.

Then the phone calls started. She was told she was not fit to be a mother. Did she know there were people in this world who had never been blessed with children? There were proper married couples who would give anything to have children, who would know how to love them, how to care for them. She was not fit to be left in charge of a dog. She was called a tart and a slut. They never gave their names. There was so much hate in their voices. She had to get Dora to answer the phone for her.

'You ought to be ashamed of yourself,' Dora said and slammed the phone down.

The police arranged for her to be given an ex-directory number and the calls stopped.

5

'If someone wants to smoke in our house,' said Pris Hodge, 'we just rush them straight out into the garden, don't we?'

'We certainly do, darling,' said Derek. 'Straight out of the house and into the garden.'

Pris and Derek were sitting side by side at the table. Val and Cathy sat opposite them. Norman was sitting opposite

Don Prewitt. They had finished dinner and Val had lit a cigarette. She took another puff. The smoke drifted across the table towards Pris.

'John used to smoke cigars,' said Cathy Pelham. 'I rather miss the smell.'

'Oh God,' said Derek, 'foot in it again. Derek does it again. Sorry, Cath.'

'No, no,' Cathy said, 'you're quite right. It is anti-social, I suppose.'

Val smiled, but this time she blew her smoke up towards the ceiling.

Norman was glad he didn't smoke. He was feeling uncomfortable enough already. Val didn't seem at all bothered, though since she was in her own house and she had just given them a very good dinner she could presumably blow as much smoke around as she liked.

He hadn't expected so many people. When Val had invited him she hadn't said who else was coming and he'd half thought they might be alone, which was a nice idea while it lasted. It had turned out to be quite a gathering. Besides Norman and Val, there was Don Prewitt, the Hodges, and Cathy, who was Val's next-door neighbour.

At least he knew most of them. He knew Don and Derek from school, and Pris had been on the interviewing panel when he'd applied for the job. Cathy had introduced herself, with the air of someone who thought that such confessions were best got out of the way sooner rather than later, by announcing that her husband had just left her for another woman. Then she had said nothing for the rest of the evening until she admitted that she missed the smell of cigars.

Norman hated dinner parties, especially when the people present knew one another better than he knew any of them. He didn't know why he'd been invited. He was probably just there to make up the numbers. Two unattached women, two unattached men. Don's wife was an invalid and didn't socialize. Apparently, nobody had seen her for years. (Val had told him once that there were two theories about Sally Prewitt. Either she was a lunatic and Don had her locked in the attic, or he'd strangled her and buried her in the garden. Opinion in the staffroom was divided. 'Aren't we lovely people?' Val had said. 'Aren't you glad you joined this school?')

Val offered coffee and liqueurs. Don opted for coffee and a brandy, Norman for just coffee. Pris and Derek were staying with the wine and had opened another bottle.

'This Bulgarian stuff's quite drinkable, really,' said Pris, 'for the price.'

Val put her cigarette out and went through into the kitchen to make coffee.

'What's she on?' said Derek, when she was out of the room. 'Forty a day?'

'At least,' said Pris.

'She'll get cancer, of course,' said Derek. 'Lungs, throat, stomach, any combination you like. Breast off by the time she's forty. Heart disease. Dead by fifty. It's well enough documented. I was reading a very good article just the other day. I don't know why people do it.'

'It's suicidal,' said Pris.

'Homicidal,' said Derek. 'We're sucking the stuff in, you realize that.'

'I see they haven't found that little girl yet,' said Don, shaking his head. 'Dreadful business.'

'Dreadful,' said Norman.

Val came back with the coffee.

'Shall we have these over the fire?' she said.

They went through into the living-room and settled themselves into the sofa and armchairs. Val poured coffee for Don and Norman and herself. Don sipped his brandy. Derek and Pris had brought their bottle of wine with them.

Val collected her ashtray and sat down cross-legged on the floor beside Norman's chair.

'The mother works at the school, of course,' Don said. 'Did you know, Norman?'

'Catering,' said Derek.

'Yes, I know,' said Norman. 'Val was telling me the other day. It happened practically outside, didn't it?'

'I feel awful about it,' said Val. 'She might have been to the door and I didn't hear her. I did go upstairs for a minute.'

'That poor woman,' said Cathy. 'The state she was in. I just didn't know what to do.'

'I thought it was funny she was late,' said Val. 'I said to you, didn't I?'

'I just didn't know what to do for her,' said Cathy. 'The police took ages.'

'Have you seen her at all, Val?' said Don. 'Since . . .'

'I dropped by once. I didn't stay. Her mother was there.'

'I nearly went round myself,' said Don. 'One doesn't want to intrude, of course. She's not a church-goer, is she? It's so difficult to give comfort when people . . . People can be quite resentful, you know.'

'They're always terribly close-knit, aren't they?' said Pris. 'That sort of family.'

'There was a lot of stuff in the papers about the mother,' said Derek. 'Single parent. Men in and out of the house all the time. Kiddy out on the streets. Still, you never know what to believe.'

'It's not easy bringing a child up on your own,' said Cathy.

'Oh God,' said Derek, 'quite right, Cath. Absolutely. I don't know how they manage.'

'You wouldn't believe the trouble I have with Alex, going on about his father all the time.'

'Absolutely.'

There was a pause while Val refilled the coffee cups. Don still had most of his brandy left. The Hodges refilled their glasses.

'Derek's been telling me about all the disruption,' said Pris, 'with the police all over the school.'

'It's been terrible,' said Don, 'absolutely impossible. We haven't had classes running normally for a single day. The pupils have loved it, of course. It's been a nightmare for the rest of us.'

'I was glad to see the back of them,' said Derek, 'I can tell you.'

'I'm afraid we haven't seen the back of them by any means.' Don drank some of his brandy. 'I had a long talk with one of them. An inspector, I think he was. He was very candid. They're under a lot of pressure with this case. They assume the child is dead. They've got to find her body and then they've got to get a conviction. You know the sort of outcry there's been. It's nothing to what there'll be if they find her dead.'

'They can't think anybody at the school is involved?' said Derek.

'That's not the point,' Don said. 'They think whoever took her must have been watching her for some time, possibly watching the primary school. We're right across the road. The mother works there. Most of us have probably seen the child without knowing who she was. No, I'm afraid we haven't seen the last of the police by a long way.'

Norman had hardly taken part in this conversation. He sat nursing his coffee. The truth was that he had rather enjoyed the disruption, but he couldn't very well say so. Besides, he was watching, watching Don and Derek and Pris, and listening. They all had something he didn't have, something perhaps that he would never have. They were comfortable in front of a class. The pupils respected them – or if they didn't they pretended to, which amounted to the same thing.

44

It was not that they were particularly imposing. Derek was shorter than him by several inches and thinner and he had a bald patch the size of a saucer, though he was still under forty. His chin wasn't so much receding as in full retreat. Pris was even smaller with a pinched face and glasses and a permanent expression of disapproval. She looked like a very intelligent poodle that had just smelt something beneath its dignity. Don was tall and stooped, but he always made Norman think of a brigadier ordering his troops into battle in the wrong direction.

The fact remained that the pupils took one look at them and did what they were told. They took one look at him and did whatever they liked.

'I find it beyond belief,' Don was saying, 'utterly beyond belief. We have to suppose this child has been abducted for – what? – some kind of sexual assault? Probably murdered? It's beyond belief. You know, I really do think there's such a thing as pure evil at work in the world. We talk nowadays as if people were just morally confused, muddled up. God knows, enough people are. But there's such a thing as pure evil.'

This damped down the conversation a bit. Val lit a cigarette and shuffled closer to Norman's chair. She glanced up at him and gave him a mischievous smile. Pris picked up the bottle of wine and poured herself another glass. Derek pushed his empty glass across the floor towards her but she ignored him.

'That's absolute rubbish,' she said. 'You talk as if ninety-nine per cent of the population were perfectly ordinary, decent people and the only explanation for the other one per cent is that they're agents of the Devil.'

'I don't think I mentioned the Devil, actually,' said Don. 'But certainly I believe most people are decent.'

'That's the trouble with people like you,' said Pris. 'You think child abuse is some sort of aberration. You sit in your

45

office all day. You don't talk to these kids. Open your eyes.
I have to talk to people. I talk to the kids. I talk to the
mothers. You wouldn't believe what goes on on that estate. Dad bashes Mum around. Mum goes into hospital to
get her jaw wired up. So now the bed's empty and Dad uses
the oldest daughter instead. I see it every day, don't I?'

'You certainly do, darling.'

'Every day?' said Val. 'How dreadful for you.'

Norman couldn't see Val's face but he saw the expression on Pris's. He hadn't realized until that moment that
they couldn't stand each other.

'Oh, come on,' Don said, 'that's outrageous. Of course I
talk to families. I see parents all the time. I talk to all sorts
of people at the church. I can't accept that.'

'Do you really believe in evil?' Val said. 'Real fire and
brimstone stuff? It's not all society's fault?'

'Some things are society's fault. Certainly they are. But I
also think there's such a thing as evil. What do you think,
Norman?'

There was an expectant pause during which everyone
looked at Norman. He had been contemplating the bone
structure of Val's neck. She had a long neck, perfectly
white. He spluttered a bit and wished he hadn't opted to
go on to coffee.

'Norman, another cup?' Val said, as if she hadn't heard
the question. 'Don, another?'

'No, thank you,' said Don.

'That would be lovely,' said Norman.

She got up from the floor and went towards the door.
She turned in the doorway.

'How are you getting on at school?' she said. 'We're not
being too horrible to you?'

'Fine,' Norman said. 'Everyone's being very nice.'

'The egregious Potter seems to have taken quite a shine
to you,' said Derek.

'George the atavism,' said Pris.

'He's just trying to be helpful, I think,' Norman said. 'He is a bit old-fashioned. We don't always see eye to eye.'

The subject had now been firmly changed, thanks to Val, and Norman's lack of theological opinions was forgotten. Why had she done it? Because she thought the conversation was coming too much on to the boil, or because she thought he needed rescuing? He hoped it was the latter.

'He's out of the ark,' said Pris. 'That man is dangerous. Somebody like that can ruin a whole department.'

'He's very experienced,' said Don. 'You have to give him that.'

'Have you talked to him, Don?' said Pris. 'I did ask you. You really must, you know. Make him see reason. He must be aware of the problem, himself. He can't be happy with things the way they are.'

'I have had a word with him, as a matter of fact, but I don't see there's much I can say. All one can accuse him of is being out of sympathy with the philosophy of the department.'

'The philosophy of the county,' said Pris.

'The philosophy of the profession,' said Derek.

'We're all pupil-centred now, Don,' said Pris, 'as you know. I mean, everybody is. George is just totally teacher-centred. He's dreadfully chalk-and-talk. Interaction, forget it. He's just into dominance.'

'Do you mean whips and things?' said Val, coming back into the room with the coffee pot. 'I'd never have guessed.'

'Derek was sharing a classroom with him last week,' said Pris, ignoring the interruption. 'You wouldn't believe what was on the board.'

'You certainly wouldn't,' said Derek.

'Derek would swear it was Latin.'

'I certainly would.'

'I don't suppose he was teaching them Latin as such,' said Norman. 'He thinks it's important to use words accurately, so he says. I suppose that's where the Latin comes in.'

Derek snorted and helped himself to another glass of wine. Val poured coffee for herself and Norman and sat down.

'Words don't mean what they mean in Latin,' said Pris. 'Besides, the problem with these kids isn't teaching them to use language accurately. It's getting them to use it at all. The parents don't talk. They just watch television and grunt at each other. Have you ever been in the shops on the estate? Have you listened to these people? The danger with these kids is that they'll lose language altogether.'

'I think George is far too prescriptive,' said Norman.

'It's hard enough,' said Pris, 'to get them to say anything beyond "yeah" and "nah" without that old dinosaur telling them they have to know the bloody Latin before they open their mouths.'

'I can see,' said Don, 'that there's a real conflict of philosophies here. I agree that's damaging to a department, but I don't see what I can do. I think it's more Derek's problem than mine.'

'Offer him thirty-eightieths,' said Pris.

'Good heavens, Pris, I can't tell a teacher to take early retirement. I mean, short of immorality there are no grounds –'

'Offer it,' said Pris. 'I can square it with the county. He might jump at it.'

'I don't think he will,' Norman said.

'I want him out,' Pris said. 'Out, out, out. I don't care how. I just want rid of him.'

'You sound as if you want him humanely put down,' said Val.

Pris glared at her.

'The professional equivalent would do,' she said.

'Look, I really must be going,' said Cathy, standing up and looking apologetic. It took everybody by surprise because it was practically the first thing she'd said since dinner. 'Don't let me spoil things. It's Alex. He'll watch television all night if I'm not there to put my foot down.'

Norman had got the impression that she'd been nervous and uncomfortable all evening. He didn't think the others had noticed. Perhaps she was thinking about her husband, or her son, or the little girl who was missing. Or perhaps she was just feeling out of her depth. He tended to forget that there are people who think schoolteachers are intellectuals.

Norman and Don stood up.

'Is that the time?' said Don, looking at his watch.

Pris glanced up briefly and then reached for the wine bottle, helping herself to the last glass.

'And we've been talking shop all evening and boring you silly,' said Val.

'No, not at all. It was lovely. It's just Alex. He's being so difficult at the moment.'

She went out into the hall. Val and Norman went with her. Norman hovered beside her as she put her coat on and then they shook hands.

'So nice to meet you at last, Norman,' she said. 'Alex has talked so much about you.'

Alex has done what? Who the hell is Alex? Oh my God, she's a parent. He should have realized. He hadn't taken any notice of her surname when they were introduced. It was all he could do to remember first names. He obviously taught her son. There were so many of them. He looked at her to see if he was struck by a family resemblance. He wasn't.

'He's a pleasure to teach,' he said.

'I'll tell him you said so.'

Never mind who he was. What had the little monster been saying? Nothing to Norman's credit, that was for sure. This woman was presumably aware that his lessons were not models of classroom control, and now she was about to say so in front of his head of department, the headmaster and the county adviser. She was standing there, still holding on to his hand and smiling at him.

'He does seem to enjoy your lessons,' she said. 'They seem to be so lively.'

'I suppose we do get a bit boisterous sometimes.'

'Not too boisterous, I hope, Norman,' said Don, who had also come through into the hall in search of his coat.

'You're not leaving too, Don?' said Val.

'I must, I'm afraid. Sally gets so anxious if I'm not back.'

'I ought to be going too,' said Norman. 'I've got piles of marking for tomorrow.' This wasn't true, but he wanted to get away before there was any more discussion of the liveliness of his classes or before it became obvious that the experience of teaching young Alex – delightful though it was – was one of which he had absolutely no recollection.

He and Don stuck their heads back round the living-room door and said their goodbyes to the Hodges, who were obviously staying on for a while. They lived just a couple of streets away from Sefton Road. Norman and Don said their thank-yous to Val and then saw Cathy to her front door. They could hear the television from the street. Young Alex, whoever he was, was making the most of his freedom.

'You do understand,' said Don, as they stood shaking hands at the gate after Cathy had gone inside, 'that what you heard tonight is strictly confidential. About any differences of opinion in the department, I mean.'

'Of course,' Norman said.

'Such a delicate business. A word in the wrong place . . .'

Norman understood. It would do his career no good to warn George that the knives were out.

6

Alex had planned his trip to Gatehouse Road with some care. From the moment Midgeley had told him where his father was living, he had known he would have to go. His parents were both being stupid. They were obviously incapable of sorting things out for themselves, so things would have to be sorted out for them. He was sure that if he could just talk to his father, he could persuade him to see sense and come home. Besides, he was curious about the slag.

He'd decided it would be necessary to take a day off school. If he'd disappeared for an afternoon at the weekend, his mother would have insisted on knowing where he'd been. Since his father left home she had been watching him like a hawk. He could always make up a story, but there was a danger she'd check up on it. If she thought he was at school there would be no awkward questions, though it might be best to have a story ready just in case.

It probably wouldn't take a whole day, but a day was actually safer than half a day. If you were absent in the morning and turned up in the afternoon, they tended to notice. If you had the whole week off they tended to notice. A day was pretty safe. They assumed you'd been ill and somebody else had checked up on it. People got away with it all the time.

He chose a Wednesday, which was a good day because they had a change of teacher every period and they didn't have the same teacher twice. Nobody would bother about someone being absent for one period. He left for school at the normal time, taking his homework books with him – which meant he had to lug them round with him all day –

and set off on his normal route until he was out of sight of any neighbours who might be hanging about in Sefton Road. Then he veered off in the other direction and walked quickly so as not to meet anybody he knew on their way to school.

He had looked up Gatehouse Road in the *A to Z*. It was quite a long way, but he decided to walk rather than take a bus to pass the time. He couldn't show his face back home before four o'clock. He was also bothered about being conspicuous. A boy in school uniform walking around with a bag of books in the middle of the morning was suspicious. If he was sitting on a bus, people had more time to look at him and wonder what he was doing. They might ask him where he was going. Adults think they have the right to ask you anything.

By the time he was half-way to Gatehouse Road, he had decided that there was definitely something funny going on. He was sure he had seen people he recognized, people who looked like teachers from the school. They would disappear round corners as he came up to them or pass him by quickly on the other side of the road without looking at him. Could they have realized already that he wasn't in school and come out searching for him? They were probably working in teams, each team following him for a while and then handing over to the next. He'd read somewhere what you were supposed to do in this situation.

He began noticing everyone who went past, looking at their faces, their clothes, so that he would know if he saw the same person twice. That would be conclusive. He began turning corners suddenly and doubling back, anything he could think of to frustrate his pursuers. His tactics became more and more complicated until he was going up and down streets in all directions. Even so, it was only a little after ten o'clock when he reached Gatehouse Road.

He was in an area of the town he hardly knew. It looked run down and disreputable. Gatehouse Road was a turning off a seedy-looking main road full of junk shops and charity shops and places advertising take-away food. Alex turned the corner and began walking along the road, looking up at the houses.

Here was a problem he hadn't really thought about. He'd thought a lot about how to get the day off school and how to get here, but he hadn't thought about what to do when he arrived. He didn't know the address. He'd just assumed that when he got here something would happen. Perhaps he would see his father. Perhaps he would see the slag, though he had no way of recognizing her if he did. He was sure something would happen to tell him where to go. At least he knew he was looking for a flat. Midgeley had definitely said it was a flat.

The whole road was flats. It was a long, narrow road with terraces on both sides, all divided up into flats. Each front door had about half a dozen bells with a piece of card beside them with names on telling you which bell to ring. Sometimes there were no names, just Flat A, Flat B. He went into a few of the gardens and read the names. The gardens were overgrown with weeds or full of rubbish and the doors had paint peeling off. There didn't seem to be any people in the houses – a lot of the curtains were still drawn – or if there were, they didn't take any notice of him going in and out of gardens and peering at front doors.

He went back to the main road and into a bread shop that had tables in the corner where they did coffee and sandwiches. This wasn't very sensible – he was making himself conspicuous again – but the people in the shop were talking or reading newspapers and they didn't seem to be taking any notice of him. They might just have been pretending, of course. Better not stay too long. He had a cup of coffee and a bag of crisps and thought about his next move. He didn't like coffee and he never drank it at home, but it seemed the right thing to drink on a mission like this.

He went back to Gatehouse Road and walked up and down again, up one side of the road to the end and then down the other side. Every three or four houses, he went into the garden and up to the front door and read the names on the bells. There were no Pelhams. He wondered if he should ring one of the bells and ask. He didn't want to get into conversation, to have to explain what he was doing. This was private business and it seemed wrong to involve strangers even by just asking questions. But if he didn't ask, he had no chance at all of finding out where his father was.

He was beginning to realize that he had come very badly prepared and that this was going to be a longer operation than he'd imagined. He wasn't going to get it done in one day. There wasn't much more he could do on his first visit than reconnoitre the territory. He decided to try one house. He went up to the door and rang one of the bells. Nobody answered. He waited. Still no answer. He'd done what he had to do. He couldn't help it if there was nobody in. He really hadn't thought enough about this. A lot more planning was called for.

A woman came walking up from the main road carrying a shopping bag. She turned and smiled at him as she went past. She was about his mother's age but there was something about her that made her different from his mother or any of the women teachers at school. Her clothes looked old and they were too tight. There was something funny about the way she smiled at him, as if she knew who he was. He wished he'd looked up 'slag' in the dictionary before he came out, then he would have known exactly what he was looking for.

He let her get a little way ahead of him and then he followed her, strolling along casually and pretending to look up at the houses but really looking at her. Her skirt was definitely too tight at the back and she was wearing the sort of make-up his mother wore when she was going out for the evening. He noticed that the hand holding the shopping bag had rings on the thumb and the index finger but she didn't seem to have a wedding ring. She was certainly what his mother would have called a bit rough. No question about that. In fact, the closer he looked at her the slaggier she seemed.

She turned into one of the gardens and went down a flight of steps. He slowed down and then, when he reached the gate, he saw her letting herself into a basement flat. He walked on past the gate, then turned round and came back.

He spent a long time hovering outside the gate, wondering whether to go in. Finally he plucked up courage and set off down the steps. There was a window below him and he could see the woman inside. She was in the kitchen unpacking her shopping. He crept down the last few steps towards the door. He couldn't see anyone else in the kitchen, only the woman with the shopping. She looked up and saw him.

Alex was back on the main road. He looked round. Nobody was following him. She was probably the wrong woman anyway. Just a woman out shopping. He had to admit defeat. Well, not completely. At least he knew where the road was and he'd identified his main problem. It was a start, but he would have to do a lot more planning before he came out here again.

The rest of the day was horrible. It still wasn't even lunch time. It was hours before he could go home. He spent half an hour looking in shop windows on the main road and then he went back to the bread shop and looked in the window. There were different people inside now, so he went in and had another cup of coffee and a sandwich. He ate his sandwich as slowly as he could but it was still only twelve o'clock when he came out of the bread shop.

He spent the next few hours wandering around the town. It was very boring. He would have liked to go into a cinema but he only passed one and it didn't have a film he was allowed to see on his own. He sat in a park. He wished he hadn't had his uniform on and his bag of books with him. He was sure everybody was staring at him. He remembered his pursuers and began looking at faces again. Best to keep moving, walk quickly, look as if he was going somewhere in a hurry, on serious business.

At half-past three he was back at the school. He couldn't make his walk last any longer and he didn't know where else to go. It was still too early to go home. He was tired and hungry and his feet hurt. There didn't seem to be anybody about. Everyone was still in class. He went in the back door of the school and crept along one of the corridors and into the toilets. He went into one of the cubicles, bolted the door and sat there reading the graffiti on the walls.

This hadn't been such a good idea. It gave him a chance to stop walking and sit down, which was all that had mattered when he came in, but now he was stuck here. It was getting on for four o'clock. If he came out during the end-of-school rush, he was bound to meet somebody from his class and he'd have to explain where he'd been all day. Something else had occured to him. It would be suspicious if he went home with exactly the same books he'd had the evening before. His mother had started supervising his homework.

The bell rang for the end of school. Alex sat tight in his cubicle. At first, nothing happened. Then, within a couple of minutes, it sounded as if the whole school was just outside. Somebody banged on the door. The cubicles on either side of him were now noisily occupied. Probably they all were. Alex sat there and waited for the noise to stop. It seemed to go on for ever. Ten minutes passed, fifteen minutes. It was quieter now but there were obviously still people about. Just when he thought it was safe, somebody banged on the door again.

'Who's in there?'

When all the noise had stopped, he gave it a few more minutes and then he came out. He was alone. His plan was to go into the classroom where his desk was, get rid of the books he had with him and collect some new ones to take home. He came out of the toilets and began walking down the corridor towards the classroom. If anybody stopped him, he would say he'd been on his way home and he'd forgotten something.

'I'll tell you a good one,' George said. 'You're at the front of the class handing back the homework, right?'

'Right,' said Norman. He was looking uneasy already. Somebody had been having a word with him.

'OK. What you do is you get them to come up one at a time to collect it. Now, chummy has been giving you a bit of trouble. When he comes up to the front, you're handing him his stuff and you accidentally drop it on the floor. Chummy bends over to pick it up. Wham! Flat of the hand on the back of his neck from a great height.'

'You can't do that, George.'

'I kid you not. Knocks them silly for the rest of the hour.'

'It's illegal, George. They can sue you for damages.'

Norman couldn't teach his way out of a paper bag, bless him, but he knew what was legal and what wasn't.

'Do you know my greatest regret?' George said. 'No more chalk. Have you ever tried throwing a whiteboard marker? Useless. You can't aim the bloody thing. Now, a piece of chalk is another story. Bounce it off the lid of the desk. Catch him under the chin with the ricochet. Lethal.'

'Could I have a word, Mr Potter?' Don Prewitt had come sneaking up behind them. He was making a habit of it.

'Any time, Don.'

'My office, Mr Potter?'

'I'm on my way, Don.'

This time the tea and biscuits remained in the cupboard. This was business. Don kept his jacket on.

'I've been thinking about you, George,' he said.

'Really?'

It wasn't that George disliked the headmaster. He was quite fond of him. Don was very big on the Christianity, of course, which George didn't have any time for. George was what you might call a lapsed humanist. He suspected that, purely in terms of the argument, Prewitt would have been on his side against the Hodges. The headmaster's problem was that he hated conflict. The Hodges ran the department and George was in a minority of one, so the Hodges had to have their way.

'Twenty-nine years, is it?' said Don, with a rather unconvincing mixture of admiration and astonishment.

'That's right.'

'It's a long time, George.'

'Never a dull moment, Don.'

'There must be times, though, George. There must be times . . .'

'Oh, there are times, Don.'

And I can keep this up, thought George, until the cows come home. If you think I'm helping you get to the point, think again.

'You'll be looking forward to your forty-eightieths.'

'It's a long way off yet,' George said. Forty-eightieths was school-speak for a full pension, half a salary after forty years' service. George had eleven years to go.

'People have been known to go early,' Don said.

Oh, have they now?

'There was Bob Petty last year,' Don said. 'He was on twenty-nine like you. The county made it up to thirty.'

'He was supposed to be ill,' George said.

'Burn-out,' Don said. 'That's right. It's not uncommon these days. The county are very sympathetic.'

Burn-out? This sounded a bit over the top. George had not thought of himself as burnt out. Fed up, at times. Pissed off, now and again. Burn-out sounded a bit strong.

'Bob was desperate,' he said. 'He couldn't control a class any more. He just stood there and gibbered. They were having him for breakfast.'

'It affects people differently. Think about it, George. Talk it over with . . .'

George allowed a sufficiently long pause to make it clear that the headmaster could not have completed the sentence if they'd stood there all day.

'Audrey,' he said.

'Audrey,' said Don, as if it had been on the tip of his tongue. 'Talk it over with Audrey.'

'We're divorced.'

'So you are. Well, think about it. Think about thirty-eightieths, George.'

George had already thought about it. This was not Prewitt's idea. A man who was devious enough to come up with this little tactic for getting an awkward teacher out of the way would have taken the trouble to check the name of his wife. This was the Hodges' work.

Come to think of it, burn-out sounded quite fun. It gave scope for all kinds of subversion. Burn-out they wanted, burn-out they were going to get.

On his way back to the staffroom from the headmaster's office, George spotted one of the second-formers creeping about in a classroom where he had no business being. His first thought was to ignore it, but then he decided he deserved a treat.

'*Name*?' he said, in his best flay-the-wits-out-of-them voice. The poor little devil nearly jumped out of his skin. George was feeling better already.

Five minutes later, young Master Pelham had received the roasting of his life and George was feeling very much better.

The feeling didn't last long. When he got back to the staffroom to pick up his briefcase before going home, Derek Hodge was in there reading the newspaper.

'Everything all right?' he said, looking at George over the top of his paper.

'Pardon?'

'I noticed you were in with Don.' He smiled. 'Everything all right?'

Derek was one of those people who are at their most unpleasant when trying to be pleasant. Fortunately, where George was concerned, he didn't try very often.

'Fine, thanks,' said George. 'Everything's fine. We have these little chats from time to time. Don't you?'

The smile disappeared and Derek's head bobbed down behind the newspaper. He wasn't really reading it any more because the pages weren't turning. He was working up to something. George fiddled with his briefcase and waited.

'I was hoping to have a word, actually,' Derek said, folding his paper and putting it down. His voice shook slightly.

'Oh, yes?' Now, what could this be about? Had Derek too detected signs of burn-out? Was it the talk of the staffroom?

'Young Norman,' said Derek. 'You seem to have, well, taken him under your wing.'

'I wouldn't say that, exactly. I try to keep him straight.'

'Is that what you think you're doing?'

George had been expecting this. His advice to Norman on the finer points of classroom practice could not have gone unnoticed.

'I think we senior members of staff have an obligation, don't you?'

'Stop it,' said Derek. 'That's all I've got to say. Just stop it.' He picked up his newspaper again.

'Really, Derek, I –'

'Just stop it, that's all.'

Derek's head disappeared behind the newspaper again but he still wasn't turning the pages, and George noticed that his hands were shaking. He was furious.

This was something that George had noticed about him before. He didn't know how to get angry in public. He had no way of expressing anger face-to-face. He didn't sulk. It was much stronger than that. He seethed quietly. George knew the sort of things Derek said about him behind his back. He obviously spent a lot of his time seething, especially when George was around. It must be awfully bad for him.

'Really, Derek,' George sat down in one of the armchairs, 'I don't know what you mean.'

'Yes, you do,' from behind the newspaper. 'Oh, yes, you do.'

He was completely incapable of losing his temper and having a proper row. He didn't have any language for it. Maybe it was the experience of living under Pris's thumb. George remembered that the pupils were more frightened of Derek than they were of him. George bit their heads off and then forgot about it, but Derek got even. He was all palsy-walsy in class and they didn't know when they'd offended him. He said nothing, waited his chance and got his revenge.

61

'Maybe I'm being a bit slow here,' said George, 'but I'm afraid you're going to have to spell this out for me.' This wasn't as much fun as a good blazing row with Pris but it had a charm of its own.

'You know. You know what you're doing.'

'With Norman, you mean? I'm just trying to keep him straight. Benefit of experience, sort of thing.'

The newspaper was lowered a few inches and Derek looked at him pop-eyed over the top.

'I've told you. Just stop it.'

If it hadn't been well after four o'clock, George might have kept this going for a while to see just what sort of state Derek would get himself into, but still being on the premises after four o'clock was not a situation he took lightly.

'Oh, I can't be bothered with this,' he said. He stood up and picked up his briefcase. 'I've got enough trouble with inarticulate kids without coping with inarticulate English teachers. If you've got something to say, put it in writing.'

As George went out of the staffroom, Derek was back behind his paper again. The pages quivered in his hands.

As he walked home, Alex decided that now he really did hate George Potter more than absolutely anybody else in the whole world. The other thing on his mind was that he was late. He'd spent the whole day worrying in case he got home suspiciously early, and now he was going to have to explain why he was late.

When he got back to the lanes, something had been going on. At the point where the lane nearest his house came out into the street, there were bunches of flowers lying on the pavement. A fluffy toy, still in its cellophane wrapper, was propped up against the wall. He stood and looked at them for a while and then went into the house. He needn't have worried about the time. His mother was out.

He made himself a sandwich, and at five o'clock he switched on the television news. They'd found the little girl. Somebody walking his dog had found her body on a piece of waste ground. There were pictures of the place. He recognized it. It was only a couple of miles away.

The police said that she'd been bound and gagged and strangled. She was fully clothed but there was evidence . . .

He listened to the end of the bulletin and then switched off and went up to his bedroom to look at his dictionary. He knew what 'penetration' meant but he needed to look up 'vaginal' and 'anal'.

7

Daisy's funeral was held on the Sunday following the discovery of her body. It rained all day. A lot of the neighbours from the estate were there and some of the teachers and all the catering staff from the school. The press still outnumbered the mourners. Daisy's father came over from Germany. He and Sarah managed to avoid each other for most of the day. When avoidance was impossible, they talked politely about his new family. Sarah's father came, but he was only allowed to spend one night before Dora sent him back home.

The press and television interest was intense. Sarah again failed to do herself credit in front of the cameras. She was repeatedly asked if she hated Daisy's killer. She said she didn't know. This was unacceptable. Dora said he should be strung up.

The story of the funeral led the television news that evening and was on most of the front pages the following morning. Daisy was now the most famous person in Britain. People had heard of her who could not have identified the Prime Minister. It was enough to mention her name and they would shake their heads and say how terrible it was and that they didn't know what the world was coming to. She had become part of the evidence for those who believe in the peculiar barbarity of our times. There were civil wars with neighbour fighting neighbour, there were famines with matchstick children every night on the news, and now there was Daisy.

She was no longer Daisy but DAISY, no longer an individual child but a symbol, an issue, a focus of unnameable anger and pity and fear. She had been blanched of all individuality. If the real flesh-and-blood Daisy had had a personality of her own, if she had ever been naughty or petulant, if she had ever driven her mother to tears, if she had ever shown flashes of precocious intelligence, if she had had her moments of triumph over the adult world, all this was forgotten. The new Daisy was an icon of innocence, the universal child, the embodiment of goodness.

She could only have been destroyed by the embodiment of evil. Somewhere, in the next house, on the next street, there was a beast, a monster to be found. People who had never known Daisy appeared on television to say that when he was caught they would find some way to kill him. Violent criminals serving prison sentences for causing misery and destruction of every kind asked for nothing more than to be alone with him in a cell.

Chief Inspector Rosewall asked for two things. First, let them find him before he struck again. Second, please God don't let him be mentally defective, don't let him belong to an ethnic minority, and don't let him confess in the back of a police car. Before you could say 'miscarriage of justice', his old mum would have been wheeled on sobbing her heart out, somebody would have done a programme about it on television, all the weirdos in the country would have signed a petition, the Court of Appeal would have chucked it out, and they'd be back at square one.

Square one was where they were at the moment. There was nothing wrong with that. Nothing wrong with square one. You have to start at square one to get to square two. That's what the public didn't understand.

The answer to 'And what are the police doing about it?' was simple and specific. They were doing what they always do. They were going methodically through the procedure. They had been over the scene of the crime and picked it clean of every scrap of information it had to offer. They had been from house to house looking for the one person, and there's always one, who had seen something and didn't know he'd seen it. They'd checked Daisy's murder, detail for detail, against similar crimes. It took time, but there was no other way of doing it.

And they had one good, solid piece of evidence. Something they could take into a courtroom. It was no use to them until they had a suspect, but the time would come when it would be vital.

It wasn't that the inspector was any less affected by Daisy's death than anyone else, but it wasn't his job to worry about what the world was coming to. It wasn't his concern whether her death was a terrible indictment of society or the government or the male sex or the human race in general. Daisy hadn't been murdered by society. She had been murdered by one person and it was the inspector's job to find him.

Daisy Beale was not the only problem on the chief inspector's mind. Sandra was being difficult again. The Rosewalls had the distinction of being the world's worst parents. They were the meanest, the strictest, their attitudes about everything were totally out of date and they never listened to a word she said.

The previous evening had been characteristically horrible. Sandra was sitting on the floor reading a magazine which seemed to consist entirely of photographs of adolescent boys with unlikely haircuts and too many teeth. She had read it cover to cover half a dozen times. This was a girl who was doing English literature A-level. Her mother asked her, innocently enough, why she never invited any of her friends home.

Sandra looked up from the magazine.

'Oh, great,' she said. 'How can I invite anybody home? How can I introduce anybody to you two? This is my dad. He's in the filth.'

'Your father,' said Miriam, 'is a senior officer in the police service.'

'That,' said Sandra, 'is what I've just said, isn't it? You don't listen.'

'You don't have to tell them the truth,' said Rosewall. 'Tell them I'm anything you like.'

'Great,' she said. 'How can I invite anybody here? Look at this house.'

'What's wrong with the house?' said Miriam.

'It's gross, Mum,' she said, and returned to her magazine.

It had not always been like this. It had started when she went into the sixth form. Even since, there had been times when she was bordering on civilized, but not recently.

The other constant source of conflict, apart from the unacceptability of her home and her parents, was money. What had put her in a bad mood was that Rosewall had turned down her demand for twenty pounds to go to the pictures. Her pocket money was calculated to cover anything a sixteen-year-old could reasonably want to do, short of funding a heroin addiction.

'Don't tell me,' she said. 'You and Mum used to go to the pictures, go out for a meal, take a taxi home and get change out of twenty p . It's not the sixties now, Dad.'

'It still doesn't cost twenty pounds to go to the pictures, Sandy.'

'I've got to live,' she said. 'And don't call me Sandy. It sounds like a dog. No, it doesn't. People give their dogs sensible names.'

'What's happened to your watch?' said Audrey Potter.

'It broke,' George said. 'Nothing serious. I'll get it fixed.'

He was round at his ex-wife's house for dinner. She'd been threatening to cook him a meal for months. He'd accepted the invitation because his curiosity had finally got the better of him as to whether she was still living alone. She seemed to be. He'd been up to the bathroom and poked his head round the bedroom door and there was nothing suspicious. She was either on her own or she'd done a lot of tidying up for his benefit, which would have been out of character.

'What have you done with it?' she said.

'It's in my briefcase.'

'It's not going to get fixed in there.'

'I'll get it seen to,' he said. 'I don't know how you can bother about that sort of thing when they're all out to get me. I've told you they're all out to get me.' He had been telling her about his conversation with Prewitt. 'Burn-out, that's what he said. Thirty-eightieths, George. Think about it, George.'

'Oh, for God's sake,' she said, 'nobody's out to get you. You're paranoid. You always were. You've been a thorn in their side for years. Nothing's changed.'

'Something has. He's never mentioned burn-out before. He's never offered me thirty-eightieths before. It's the bloody black spot, that's what it is.'

'Forget your eightieths,' she said. 'You've been enemies with the Hodges ever since they set foot in that school. You've all been at it for years. You just can't stand people disagreeing with you.'

'That's not true,' he said. 'I don't mind people disagreeing with me. I just wish they wouldn't say such stupid things when they do.'

'You know, there's something about me,' she said, 'that brings out the worst in you. One look at me and you start whining about something. It's all ballocks. You're enjoying yourself really.'

'No, I'm not,' he said. 'They're out to get me. You'll see. Mark my words.'

'You were with him,' his mother said. 'Don't lie to me.'

It was Monday of the week after Alex's expedition to Gatehouse Road. He'd just got in from school. She was sitting in the living-room with the door open, staring straight in front of her, not looking at him. She'd been waiting for him. She had the door open so she could hear when he came in.

Alex put his bag of books down at the door and took his jacket off slowly and came and stood in the doorway. She still didn't look at him.

'You were with him,' she said. 'Last week.'

'No, I wasn't. With who?'

'Yes, you were. With him and that slag.'

She'd obviously been crying before he came in. Now she started again, sitting rigid in the chair but covering her face with her hands.

It had all been going so well. It was nearly a week now. He thought he'd got away with it. He'd even started planning his second trip. None of the teachers had said anything to him about being absent. He'd had any number of stories ready, but none of them seemed to have noticed. His classmates had noticed, but a day's truancy seemed to have done his reputation a bit of good. They'd begun to wonder if he might be half normal after all.

He couldn't imagine how she'd found out, which made it difficult to deny because he didn't know which part of it to deny. Somebody must have seen him, but where had they seen him? He'd have to find out how much she knew. He stood just inside the doorway, looking at her.

'What do you mean?' he said. 'With Dad, do you mean?'

'Don't lie to me, Alex.'

'I'm not.'

'You weren't in school.'

Alex said nothing. He just stood looking at her, waiting for the rest of it. He needed to know exactly what she knew and how she knew it, then he could start building up a story from there.

She turned and looked at him. Her eyes were red from crying and she had that terrible look on her face, the look that told him he had betrayed her.

'It's no good lying,' she said. 'Val was in your class. She went back and checked later on. She says you were missing all day. She thought you were ill.'

He might have known Valerie Kellett would be at the bottom of it. What was she doing in his class? She didn't even teach them. She had no business being there. This was what came of people being neighbours and teachers instead of one or the other.

Two things struck him at once. Miss Kellett hadn't raised the alarm at school, either on the day he was missing or since. He was sure about that. None of the teachers had said a word to him. She'd kept it to herself and then, the next time she saw his mother, she had checked whether he was ill. Secondly, she couldn't possibly have known where he was. He would have to admit taking the day off school, but at least he didn't have to admit where he'd been.

'I wasn't with anybody,' he said.

'Tell me where you were, Alex. No lies. Just tell me where you were.'

'I just didn't go to school,' he said, 'that's all.'

'I don't believe you,' she said. 'You've never done that. You were with him, I know you were. How did he get in touch with you?' She sat forward in her chair. She wasn't crying now. Her face was hard but there was that frightened look again. 'He phoned you, is that it?'

'I don't know where he is. How could I? You won't tell me where he is. He hasn't been in touch. I swear he hasn't. It was nothing to do with him.'

She looked at him for a long time, searching his face for the truth, and then she got up from her chair and came over and put her arms round him. He buried his head in her shoulder.

'Tell me, Alex, please. Just tell me the truth. I won't be angry.' She ruffled his hair. 'I don't blame you. I just have to know.'

'I was frightened,' he said. He pulled away from her and went and sat down in the chair opposite hers. 'I was frightened to go into school.'

This was going to have to be good. Alex had been bullied a lot at school, particularly in the first year, but it wasn't so bad this year. He couldn't suddenly claim he was frightened to go into school because of that. His parents had never taken the bullying seriously, anyway. His father had told him he'd have to learn to look after himself. Besides, story-telling doesn't work that way. If you tell people something that's quite likely but just a bit untrue, they put on a clever grown-up face, cock their heads on one side and say, 'Are you telling me stories, young man?' If you tell them a real juicy whopper, they fall for it.

'It was last Tuesday,' he said. 'I was coming out of school and one of the teachers was coming out. He offered me a lift in his car.'

It was done. He had committed himself. He had committed himself to his story and he could never go back.

His mother said nothing, but the expression on her face changed completely. She came back to her chair and sat down opposite him, her eyes fixed on his face, her fingers twisting together.

'He asked me to get into his car,' Alex said, getting into his stride. He was beginning to picture the whole thing, as if it were a memory. It wasn't like a story. It seemed to be true. It had to be true. What could not possibly be true was that he had betrayed her. 'He said he'd give me a lift home. I thought it was funny. I've seen him lots of times coming out of school and he's never offered anybody a lift before. I just thought it was funny.'

'Go on,' she said.

'Well, I didn't think any more about it until the next day. I was going into school and he was standing there, just outside the gate, watching me. Sort of staring at me. I got frightened so I didn't go in. I just walked round all day.'

His mother didn't say anything for a while. She sat looking at him and then she looked down at the floor and then she looked up at him again.

'Is this the truth, Alex?'

'Yes,' he said. 'Honestly.'

'Which teacher was it? You must tell me, Alex. This is important.'

'He doesn't teach me,' he said, shaking his head and sounding puzzled, and then, as if it had suddenly occurred to him, 'I think his name's Mr Potter.'

Norman wanted to invite Val to the pub after school. He wanted a chance to get her on her own but he didn't want to make it obvious that that was what he was trying to do. He was terrified of anyone on the staff realizing that he fancied her. He hated people knowing what he was doing. He wasn't even sure if he wanted her to realize.

He'd been planning to try to get her on her own at four o'clock, but when he got back to the staffroom after his last lesson the whole staff were there. Don Prewitt had called a meeting.

Don came in just after four and apologized for keeping everyone late. He'd had a call from the police. Over the next couple of weeks, they would need to interview all members of staff individually and at length. There would inevitably be some disruption of classes.

Everybody started complaining. They'd been interviewed once already. Nobody knew anything. It was the pupils who would suffer. Even Norman had been in teaching long enough to know that most people love having their classes cancelled, but it is totally unacceptable to say so. The fiction must be maintained that if so much as an hour of teaching is lost, children's lives will be blighted for ever.

'I did make it clear to them,' said Don, 'but I'm afraid they're not interested in how much they disrupt our work. I gather that they think the little girl was taken by someone she knew. Many of us know the mother. I suppose most of us would have had an opportunity to see the little girl. I'm afraid that until this case is solved we're just going to have to put up with this sort of thing.'

There was more complaining, which went on for longer than Norman thought was necessary, and then Prewitt left and people began to drift away in ones and twos. Eventually, only Norman and Val and Derek Hodge were left in the staffroom. Derek seemed to be in no hurry to go home.

'It's all show, of course,' he said. 'I don't suppose they've got any real leads. They just have to be seen to be doing something. So they come here and turn us upside down. Somebody ought to make a complaint. I'm going to have a word with Pris.'

So, go home and have it, thought Norman.

'Let's just hope they find who did it,' he said.

'I don't care if they find somebody who didn't do it,' said Derek, 'so long as they leave us alone.'

Val was on her way to the door. Norman had a brilliant idea. He invited them both to the pub. He was pretty sure what Derek's answer would be.

'Maybe a quick one,' said Val.

'We don't go to pubs,' Derek said. 'Thanks all the same. You can never get the stink of tobacco out of your clothes. Pris wouldn't have me in the house.'

'I suppose it's just you and me, then, Val,' Norman said, trying to sound disappointed.

'You know me,' she said. 'I thrive on tobacco.'

'Last time I was in a pub,' said Derek, 'there was one of my fifth-formers in there. Pint in his hand, fag in his mouth. His parents got a letter.'

The pub was about a mile from the school. He deliberately avoided the ones the teachers used as regulars. It was also one of the few pubs left in the town that looked the way a pub should look, with heavy, dark brown furniture and deep, leather armchairs that were comfortable and could only gain in character from having beer spilt on them. Norman had a pint, Val a gin and tonic. A haze of cigarette smoke curled above their heads, hung in columns below the high ceiling and nosed into every corner of the room. Val was in her element.

She was looking particularly fetching. She was wearing her usual trouser suit over a powder-blue jumper with a neckline almost up to her ears. The rather masculine outfit suited her, but the occasional V-neck would have been appreciated. He knew she had no breasts but that didn't stop him wanting to know the precise extent to which she had no breasts. But then, when she took the jacket off and hung it over her chair, there was the delicious revelation that this particular jumper was completely sleeveless. The contrast of the bare white arms and shoulders with the severity of the neckline was particularly sexy.

'Let's not talk about school,' she said. 'I want to forget the place.'

They talked about their families. She was an only child. Norman had a sister but they weren't close. His parents were alive. Her father had died of a heart attack.

'He was in his forties when I was born,' she said. 'Mum was a lot younger than him. She remarried, so I got Sefton Road. At least I've never had to worry about a mortgage.'

'It's a big house,' Norman said.

'Too big, is that what you mean? That's what everybody says. Why don't I sell it and move into a nice cosy little flat? I'd hate it.'

'You don't feel the need for a man about the house?' he said, and regretted it immediately.

'I can do anything a man can do,' she said. 'I paint the walls, I mend the fuses, I unblock the drains. I can't stand the sort of woman who needs a man to change a light bulb.'

Happily, she had misunderstood what he thought she might need a man for. He wasn't very good at this sort of thing. He wasn't very good with women. He'd never mastered the intermediate stage between making small talk and inviting them to bed. And whatever the mysterious quality was which some men have that makes women say yes to a blunt request for sex, Norman knew he didn't have it. Women laughed at him.

He had never thought for a moment that Val was laughing at him. This was one reason he liked her. The other reason was that talking to her wasn't like talking to a woman at all. He didn't feel at all self-conscious. Women usually behaved as if they were waiting for him to impress them, at which he always failed, or waiting for him to give them a reason to make fun of him, at which he usually succeeded. Val behaved as if they were just two people out having a drink together. He felt he could have told her anything. Maybe it was because she was older.

'You must come and have a proper look round the house one day,' she said.

'That would be nice.'

She took out a cigarette. Norman picked her lighter up off the table and flicked it alight. She cupped her hand round his and guided it towards her cigarette.

That one moment of intimacy apart, the evening was not a success from Norman's point of view. The thing that most attracted him to her, the fact that she just treated him as a friend, was proving to be an impediment.

They both had marking to do and an early class in the morning. He persuaded her to have a quick final drink before they left. Val insisted on buying the round.

'So, how's it going?' she said, when she came back to the table. 'Bit better? Even worse?'

'I thought you didn't want to talk about school.'

'I'm on my second drink,' she said. 'I can just about cope with it.'

'I don't think I was cut out for this job,' Norman said.

She took a sip of her gin and a puff on her cigarette and looked at him.

'Do you know what we've all got in common?' she said. 'Teachers, I mean.'

'Overworked,' he said, 'underpaid.'

'Apart from the obvious. I mean, the sort of people we are.'

'No.'

'We're all actors. It's all play-acting, really. We've all got our roles and we slip into them each time we go into class. It's got to be something the kids can recognize. Something simple and well-defined and consistent. It's like putting on a mask.'

'I don't know what you mean,' he said.

'Look at George. George is a tartar. Cross him and you'll regret it. They don't know what would actually happen if they crossed him because nobody ever tries. Don is a stickler for the rules. Stay inside the rules and he'll never let you down. Firm but fair, that's Don.'

'What about you?' he said.

'Me? I'm the brisk, practical one. Down to business and no nonsense. None of it's true, of course. It's not really us. George is a great softy, really. Don has had real tragedy in his life.'

'What you're saying . . .' he said.

'What I'm saying is that you haven't decided what role you're playing. When you go into class, you're just yourself. What the kids are getting is something muddled, inconsistent, just the way most of us are most of the time. They don't know how to cope with it. They don't know who they're dealing with.'

'So, get myself a mask,' he said.

'Get yourself a mask, Norman. The wonderful thing is you can choose your own.'

'If it's about early retirement,' George said, 'you can –'

'It's not about that.'

'Oh?'

George had received another summons to Don Prewitt's office. The headmaster had caught him in the corridor as he was coming out of the staff meeting. He was getting tired of this. Besides, it was getting on for five o'clock and George was still on school premises. If Prewitt didn't appreciate the full horror of this fact, George did.

'I really don't know how to put this to you, George,' Don said, when they were sitting in the office with the door shut. The headmaster had made quite a rigmarole of peering up and down the corridor and shutting the door. 'It really is rather delicate. I might say very delicate, in fact.'

George was beginning to suspect that this was not to be another rambling discussion of his career prospects, or lack of. The headmaster had the sort of expression on his face which he adopted when one of his brighter boys, and a regular church-goer at that, had been caught showing an interest in female physiology behind the bike sheds.

George waited. What could he be suffering from this time? More stress? Total burn-out? Or had he reached some new stage in his relentless deterioration?

Don needed to scrutinize the files on his desk very closely before he felt able to speak.

'You don't teach 2B, George?' he said. 'I think I'm right.'

'I haven't had the pleasure.'

'Pelham. Alexander Pelham, 2B. Is it Alexander?' He looked at a file on his desk. 'Yes, Alexander.' He looked up from the file. 'Alexander Pelham, George?'

'The "Pelham" rings a bell.'

'Could you try to be precise, George.'

'I've heard the name recently.'

'How recently?'

'Oh, I don't know. Some time last week, maybe.'

'Which day?'

What the devil was all this about? George didn't have time for this. Why couldn't this man ever, just once, come straight out with it and say what was on his mind?

'Is this important, Don?'

'Bear with me, George. I'm sure this is a misunderstanding, so we do need to be absolutely clear about the facts.'

The fact that was absolutely clear to George was that he wasn't going to escape from this interrogation until he'd remembered who young Pelham was. He knew the name was familiar.

'Hang on,' he said, 'I've got him now. It was one day last week. I found him skulking about in a classroom. I don't know what he was doing but he definitely had a guilty look about him. I gave him a flea in his ear and sent him on his way.'

'Which day was this?'

'Search me.'

'It's important, George.'

George thought about it for a moment.

'All right,' he said, 'I'll tell you when it was. It was after we had our last little chat, Don. I remember I was coming out of here when I spotted him. It was the day that little girl was found. Daisy. I remember it was on the news when I got home.'

'That was Wednesday.'

'Then it was Wednesday.'

'You're sure?'

'Positive.'

'Good, George. Excellent. Now, we'll leave that to one side for the moment. I want you to cast your mind back to the previous day. That was the Tuesday.'

Oh, was it? Tuesday before Wednesday. Well, stone me.

'It's Tuesday, George. Last week. Shortly after four o'clock. You're coming out of school on your way home. You go to your car. Do you have the picture, George?'

'Vividly, Don.'

'I want you to tell me exactly what happens next.'

'I get in the car. I go home.' Have three stiff whiskies. Collapse on sofa. No, skip that bit.

'Do you think you might be leaving anything out? An incident, let's say, that might not have struck you as important?'

'Like what?'

'Did you offer anyone a lift?'

'No.'

'Let's be clear about this, George.'

'I am clear. I don't give people lifts. Well, I've given Norman a lift a couple of times, that's all. Not recently. You can ask him.'

'You didn't offer Pelham a lift?'

'Pelham? No, of course I didn't. Why should I offer that little squirt a lift?'

'I would ask you to be sure about this, George. We have to be so careful about this sort of thing. It's so open to misinterpretation.'

'What is? Do you mind telling me what you're talking about?'

'I've had a complaint from a parent.'

'Oh.' It was not the first time George had been the subject of a complaint, though it was usually to the effect that he was giving their little angels nightmares, not giving them lifts.

'I had a visit from Mrs Pelham this morning. Do you know Mrs Pelham? No, well, I suppose you wouldn't. I happen to have met her socially, so she came to me. Fortunately, she came to me, George. She might have gone to the police.'

'I haven't got the foggiest idea what you're talking about.'

'All right, George, so you say. Now, young Pelham's story is this. Last Tuesday – Tuesday, George, not Wednesday – on his way home from school, you approached him and offered him a lift in your car. "Enticed" was the word the parent used. "Enticed", George. The boy took fright, apparently, to the extent that he was afraid to come to school next day.'

'That's absolute rubbish. He's making it up.'

'So you say, George.'

'He didn't come to school next day?'

'No.'

'All right, then, I'll tell you what this is about. He was off school, was he? There you are, then. He had a day off and now he's making up stories to protect himself.'

'But you said you saw him on Wednesday.'

'Yes, I did.'

'And you reprimanded him for being in a classroom without permission?'

'Yes.'

'You're quite sure it was Wednesday?'

'Yes.'

'The day he wasn't in school?'

'It was the day I saw you. The day they found that little girl. Look, are you telling me you believe this story? Do you seriously believe I go around enticing little boys into cars? Is that what you believe?'

Prewitt had been making notes on a pad on his desk. He looked up.

'I neither believe nor disbelieve, George. All I am trying to do at this stage is to get the facts down and then we can see where we stand.'

The one occasion on which George really disliked the headmaster was when he was being fair. He was famous for being fair, like the judge who steered a middle course between partiality and impartiality.

'Oh, great,' George said, 'thank you very much. I tell you one thing and some bloody second-former tells you another and you want to get the facts down.'

Prewitt ignored this and took his time contemplating his notes. If this was supposed to be intimidating, it worked. All sorts of things were going through George's mind. Of course, the boy was telling lies to cover his truancy. Any fool could see that. Easy enough to get the truth out of him, though. Prewitt was just being pig-headed, doing it by the book, thinking of the reputation of the school.

Unless there was more to it than that. This Pelham woman knew Prewitt socially. Prewitt was an ally of the Hodges. The Hodges were out to get him. Immorality was the only real grounds. . . . He had a sudden vision of some horrible conspiracy. He remembered what he'd said to Audrey. He hadn't really meant it. He'd been provoking her. He knew it annoyed her when he talked that way. Would they really go that far? Did they want him out that badly?

Prewitt had finished with his notes.

'What I shall do, George,' he said, 'is this. I shall interview the boy in the presence of the parent and confront him with your denial. Now, if he withdraws his story, well and good. If he persists with it, I shall interview him again with the parent present and with you present. Does that seem acceptable to you?'

'I'll talk to him.'

'Absolutely not, George. Out of the question.' He leaned forward across his desk. 'I must have an assurance from you before you leave this office that you will not under any circumstances attempt to speak to the boy. I mean it, George.'

'Give me five minutes. I'll get it out of him.'

'Do you realize the seriousness of this? It was all I could do to stop the parent from going to the police. If you go near that boy, it's out of my hands.'

George realized he had to tread carefully here. There was no point in antagonizing Prewitt. He needed to get out of here and get his thoughts straight.

'All right,' he said. 'If you think it's best.'

'You'll leave it with me?'

'Yes.'

'It's for the best, George.'

A horrible thought occurred to him. How many people knew about this?

'The mother,' George said, 'has she spoken to anyone else?'

'I'm sure she hasn't. She came straight to me. The boy told her his story yesterday evening and she came to see me this morning. I stressed the need for discretion, as you can imagine.'

'Thank you.'

'We'll leave it there for the moment, then, George.'

George got up from his chair.

'As far as I'm concerned, of course,' Prewitt said as George was on his way out of the door, 'not a word of it will go beyond this office. We have to be so careful about this sort of thing, George.'

9

'So,' said Sandra Rosewall, 'have you beaten it out of anybody yet?'

She didn't even look up at him. She was lying full length on the floor in front of the fire, with her nose in a book. Rosewall had had a long day, a hard day. He had been looking forward to a bite to eat, a chance to catch up on the newspapers and an early night.

'Pardon?' he said.

'Daisy. The confession. Shouldn't you have beaten it out of somebody by now?'

'We don't do it that way any more,' Rosewall said. 'We're quite sophisticated these days.'

'That's not what I've heard.'

'What have you heard?' he said wearily. He knew the answer.

'Get hold of somebody too daft to defend himself,' she said, 'lock him up, keep him awake, fake a bit of evidence, then bash a confession out of him.' She still hadn't looked up from the book. 'That's what everybody believes.'

'Who's everybody?' he said.

'Everybody I know.'

It was not the first time they had had this sort of conversation. Rosewall had learnt to come to terms with the fact that his daughter was deeply ashamed of what he did. On top of all the other injustices which life had heaped upon her, she had a father who beat confessions out of innocent people for a living.

At first, he had tried to argue with her. He had talked to her about forensic science, about fingerprinting. He had tried to get her interested. He was wasting his breath. He had told her about blood-typing, about the possibilities of DNA profiling, about the information that could be extracted from a single human hair.

'Gross,' she said.

He had tried being angry with her. He had tried treating it as a joke. Nothing made any difference. If she had been Rosewall's generation, she would have called him a pig. The young had other words now, but the attitude was the same.

'I thought you were supposed to be under a lot of pressure to find the killer,' she said. 'That's what it says in the papers.'

'We are.'

'Well,' she said, 'beat it out of somebody. Plenty of blacks about.'

This was her other line of attack. She took it for granted that he was a racist. There was no point in arguing about that either.

'I expect we'll get around to it,' he said. 'We haven't found anybody to beat it out of yet.'

'You do understand, Alexander, that you must tell me the absolute truth?'

'Yes, sir,' said Alex.

'Of course he does,' said his mother.

Alex was looking very smart. He'd had a haircut and his jacket and trousers had been brushed. His mother was looking very smart too. She'd put her make-up on, which she didn't usually do in the mornings.

Alex was being interrogated by the headmaster. Mr Prewitt was sitting at his desk in his office at the school. Alex, who was excused classes for the morning, was sitting in front of the desk and his mother was sitting beside him. In films they always have a lamp to shine in your eyes, but Mr Prewitt didn't have a lamp.

Alex had decided he had no choice but to stick to his story. Whatever they did to him now, it couldn't be worse than having to confess to his mother that he'd been to Gatehouse Road. He'd imagined telling her. He'd seen the look on her face, heard the silence, seen her go upstairs and shut herself in the bedroom, refusing to speak to him. He didn't care what they did to him. He wasn't confessing.

He had prepared himself for his interrogation. He had imagined the scene where Mr Potter had offered him a lift in his car. He had gone over it again and again in his mind until he could see it as clearly as if he were remembering it. There was the school gate, with people rushing past him into the street. There was the car, parked at the corner.

There was Mr Potter coming towards him with a horrible, satanic grin on his face. No, this was perhaps overdoing it. He modified the grin and went over it again in his mind. He heard the words he had spoken. He heard the words Mr Potter had spoken.

He had also prepared himself by thinking about all the films he'd seen where spies were interrogated and they refused to talk. What they could do, he could do. It was his duty not to confess. He would not reveal the secret plans. He would not betray his comrades who depended on him for their lives. He didn't care if they pulled his fingernails out.

'I want you to tell me, Alexander,' said Mr Prewitt, 'in your own words, exactly what happened when you came out of school last Tuesday. Take your time.'

Alex told his story slowly and carefully. He didn't bother about trying to use the same words he'd used when he told it before to his mother. People get suspicious if you always use the same words. He just concentrated on the pictures in his mind and described the pictures. The story came out well.

When he had finished, Mr Prewitt looked at his mother and she looked at Mr Prewitt. They believed him. He could tell.

'You're quite sure, Alexander, that Mr Potter spoke to you first? He just came up to you and spoke to you?'

'Yes, sir.'

'And he invited you to get into his car?'

'Yes, sir.'

'He didn't give you any reason?'

'He asked me if I wanted a lift home.'

'And when you said no, he asked you again?'

'Yes, sir.'

'Do you know, Alexander, that Mr Potter denies that any of this ever happened?'

Alex looked bewildered.

'Of course he denies it,' said his mother.

She and Mr Prewitt exchanged looks, the way adults do when there are things to be said once the children are out of the room.

'Why didn't you say anything to your mother about this?'

'I don't know, sir.'

'It's probably my fault,' said his mother. 'I've told you what the situation is at home. I haven't been paying as much attention to Alex as I should.'

'You didn't want to worry your mother at a difficult time,' said Mr Prewitt, 'is that right?'

'Yes, sir.'

'Now, tell me what happened on the Wednesday morning.'

Alex went through a new set of pictures in his mind and told his story. He arrived at school. There was Mr Potter standing at the gate grinning at him again, staring at him. He turned and fled.

'And you spent the day walking round the town?'

'Yes, sir.'

'You didn't come back to school all day?'

'No, sir.'

'You didn't see Mr Potter again that day?'

'No, sir.'

'Where did you go?'

'I don't remember. I just walked round.'

'He was terrified,' said his mother. 'Of course he doesn't remember.'

More looks were exchanged.

'Very well, Alexander,' said Mr Prewitt. 'Now, I want you to go and wait outside for a moment and I'm going to have a few words with your mother. Will you do that?'

'Yes, sir,' said Alex. 'Thank you, sir.'

Mr Prewitt smiled at him. His mother squeezed his hand as he went past her chair. It had all been very easy, really.

The headmaster had turned out to be no more of a challenge than Midgeley.

10

At 12.47 p.m. – the time was logged – a young white male entered the offices of the transport police at the railway station. PC Conway, who was on duty alone, remained seated at his desk until he had had a good look at him.

He was in his mid to late twenties, average height, with close-cropped fair hair, and dressed in a denim shirt and jeans and an army-surplus jacket. He had an ear-ring in one ear. In spite of appearances, PC Conway decided that the man wasn't going to be any trouble. It was the type of judgement he made several times a day. He made it quickly and he was never wrong. This, he decided, was a soft man trying to look hard.

The man was standing with his hands in his pockets looking at the posters on the walls. He seemed to be in no hurry. PC Conway stood up and walked slowly towards the front of the office. The man smiled at him.

'All right?' he said.

'Can I help you?'

'D'you know about that briefcase? It's been stood there best part of a half-hour.'

'What briefcase is that?'

'Out the front. I dropped a fare off a half-hour ago. It was stood there then. Nobody near it.'

'You're reporting a suspicious package?'

'That's what I said.'

'You'd better show me.'

PC Conway used his radio to report that he was leaving the office to investigate an unattended package, and then they walked out to the concourse at the front of the station. The man, who was a minicab driver, explained that he had happened to notice the briefcase when he had dropped a passenger off at about a quarter past twelve. When he had dropped off another passenger half an hour later, it was still there.

'Probably nothing,' he said. 'Still, you can't be too careful. All these Irish.'

The briefcase was still there, in the main entrance, standing just far enough out from the side wall that people had to walk round it. One man kicked it as he went past. PC Conway knew something was wrong as soon as he saw it. It had not been left accidentally. People leave their cases under tables in the buffet or beside the magazine rack in the newsagent's, not in a doorway. Somebody could have put it down while he went to look at the departure times, but that wouldn't take half an hour. It had been deliberately placed there and left.

'Don't go near it.'

The man nodded.

'No chance,' he said.

PC Conway used his radio to call for assistance and then began directing people towards the other entrance.

It was well after four o'clock when George got to the police station. He'd been late getting to school for his first class because he had to get the bus, and then he'd been teaching all day and he couldn't get away. He'd thought of leaving it till tomorrow, then he thought it was better to get it over and done with. Then it was pouring with rain. And he'd forgotten to bring an umbrella. Oh, forget it. It was going to be one of those days. He'd have taken the car straight to the garage and got the door fixed and not bothered reporting it if it hadn't been for the insurance, and the watch.

There was a sergeant at the desk and some old girl reporting a man she'd seen hanging about near her house. It should have taken her five minutes. It took her the best part of twenty. George nearly turned round and went home. This was eating into his evening, the only part of the day that didn't belong to the school.

'My car was broken into,' he said, when it was finally his turn, 'during the night.'

The policeman nodded slowly and reached for a piece of paper.

'Radio's gone,' George said.

'Surprise me,' said the policeman.

'And some other stuff. Papers, and a wrist-watch. The watch is the only thing I'm really bothered about.'

George gave his name and address and occupation and reported the time, seven thirty that morning, that he had discovered the break-in. The car had been parked outside his house. He reported the radio and the watch as missing.

'What we'll do,' said the sergeant, 'we'll send somebody over to have a look at it. Check for prints. Some time this evening, that all right?'

'Fine,' George said. 'Thanks.'

'Won't find anything, of course. If they haven't got gloves, they pull their jumpers down over their hands, put their socks over their hands. You wouldn't believe it.'

'No,' George said.

The policeman was taking such a long time filling out his report, George felt he ought to make conversation.

'It broke a few weeks ago,' he said. 'The watch. So I stopped wearing it and shoved it in my briefcase. I've been meaning to get it mended for ages.'

The policeman stopped writing and looked up.

'Are you saying the watch was in a briefcase?'

'Yes.'

89

'And the briefcase was taken?'

'Yes. The briefcase and the radio.'

'You didn't mention a briefcase.'

'It was a very old one,' George said. 'I'm not bothered about it. I'm bothered about the watch.'

'You said something about papers,' said the policeman. 'Would that be business papers?'

'Essays, school stuff. I told you, I'm a teacher.'

'Which school would that be?'

'Weston Secondary.'

'It would say Weston Secondary on the papers, would it?'

'Some of them, I suppose. I'm not bothered about the papers. Saves me marking them.'

George smiled. The policeman didn't.

'Could you describe this briefcase?' he said.

'It's old. Brown leather. Usual sort of thing. It's got my initials on it. G. P. I usually bring it into the house in the evening but I didn't need it yesterday so I left it in the car.'

The policeman wasn't writing any of this down.

'Just wait here a minute, will you?' he said.

'I'm in a bit of a hurry, actually.'

'Just a minute.'

The policeman disappeared into an inner office. He was gone five minutes and came back with another man, an older man in plain clothes. The new one stood and looked George up and down for a long time before he said anything.

'They've got your briefcase at Central, Mr Potter.'

'Great,' George said. 'I can't believe it. Is the watch in it?'

'They've been phoning your school about it.'

'Nobody told me,' George said. 'Is the watch there?'

'I don't know anything about a watch.'

That was too much to hope for.

'Where was it found?'

'Somebody found it at the railway station, I believe. Transport had fun with it. They thought it was a bomb.'

'They didn't blow it up or anything?' George said, humorously. Well, he thought it was humorous. The policeman obviously didn't. There was no expression on his face or in his voice.

'No, nothing like that.'

'I'll pick it up tomorrow, then,' George said, 'if that's all right. The central police station, is it? The one at the town hall?'

'I'll give you a lift over there now,' the man said.

'That's very good of you but I'd rather get home, if you don't mind. It's getting a bit late. I'll pick it up tomorrow.'

'I'll give you a lift over there now.' It didn't sound exactly like a friendly offer.

When Alex got home from school, his mother was on the phone. Something was going on. She was shrieking into the phone. He spent as much time as he could taking his mac and wet shoes off and shaking his umbrella out of the front door, pretending not to be listening.

'Isn't there any way round it?' she said. 'There must be a way round it. What are they going to do, put me in prison?'

She'd wanted to keep him off school until the business with Mr Potter was settled, but Alex had insisted on going. It wasn't worth having time off school. It was so horrible going back.

She was quiet for a long time. The person at the other end was doing all the talking. She stood twisting the telephone cord into coils around her fingers.

'All right,' she said, 'but there are conditions.' She seemed to have calmed down a bit now. She looked round to see where he was. Alex wandered through into the kitchen but he left the door open.

'I'm in a position to do anything I like,' she said. 'He does it my way or not at all.' She was quiet again. Alex crept closer

91

to the door. 'One,' she said, 'he doesn't come to the house. I'll take Alex somewhere. They can meet somewhere. Two, he has to be on his own. If she's there, it's all off.'

Alex came through from the kitchen, picked up his homework books and took them upstairs to his room. He'd heard all he needed to hear.

When he came downstairs, she was sitting in the living-room with the television on. She never put the television on before dinner. She didn't look at him.

'You're going to see him,' she said. 'That's what you wanted, isn't it?'

Why was she angry with him? He hadn't arranged it.

'To see Dad?' he said. 'Great. Thanks.'

'It wasn't my idea,' she said. 'He got a court order. I'm some sort of criminal, apparently.'

'When?' he said.

'Tomorrow, after school. I'll take you. I'll drop you off somewhere. I don't know where he wants to meet you.'

She said all this without looking at him, staring at the television, as if it were somehow all his fault. He was sure she didn't know what she was watching. It was kids' television, anyway.

The policeman had hardly spoken in the car. George had chattered all the way, describing how he'd discovered the break-in, explaining why the watch was in the briefcase, saying the same things over and over again, probably sounding like an idiot. It was partly a response to the other man's silence, partly an attempt to normalize a situation that was beginning to feel distinctly odd.

It was getting on for six o'clock. George was beginning to think about his dinner. He'd been thinking about a drink for the last hour. He didn't need the briefcase this evening. If the watch was gone, which it probably was, he didn't need it at all. Why had he got into the car? Why couldn't he have insisted that, no, it wasn't convenient and he would pick the case up in the morning? He was the injured party, after all. Just because he was dealing with the police, he'd behaved like a sheep and gone where he was told.

They finally arrived at the town hall – the traffic had been awful – and parked in an underground car-park which George hadn't known was there. He was shown into the police station through a back door, and then into a room where he was left on his own with the door shut. The policeman who'd been with him hadn't said a word since they'd got out of the car.

There was a table in the room and three chairs, two on one side of the table, one on the other. Nothing else. George sat down. He stood up, paced up and down, and sat down again in one of the other chairs. If they didn't turn up with his briefcase in the next five minutes he was just going to walk out and go home, stopping for nothing and nobody unless it was liquid and alcoholic.

He had stood up again and was just about ready to leave when the door opened and in came a man he hadn't seen before and a woman, both plain clothes. The man was carrying George's briefcase, which he put down on the table. He was a big man, several inches taller than George, with shoulders that nearly filled the doorway. The woman wasn't somebody he'd choose to meet on a dark night, either.

'Wonderful,' George said. 'Thanks very much. Do I have to sign something?'

'Is this your property?' said the man.

'Yes, that's it.' George could see that the lock had been forced open. So much for the watch.

'Just check the contents for me, would you?'

The man sat down at the table. The woman picked up one of the chairs, carried it across the room and sat down just inside the door, behind George's back. George opened the briefcase and rummaged through the papers.

'The watch is gone,' he said.

The man just sat looking at him.

'There was a watch in here,' George said. 'A wrist-watch. It's gone.'

The man said nothing. George looked round at the woman. She just stared back at him. He thought of the man who'd driven him here. Another zombie. Do they have to go on a course to get like this? Presumably they were trained not to give anything away, not even the fact that their blood was circulating.

'Check the contents, would you?' the man said.

'The papers, you mean?'

The man nodded.

'I don't know exactly what was in here.'

'Check the contents for me.'

George sat down at the table, took all the papers out and started leafing through them. There were two bunches of essays done up with rubber bands, his timetable, various lesson notes, a memo to the staff from Prewitt – nothing he would have minded losing. There was also a brown envelope which he didn't remember putting in there. He looked inside. There were photographs in it.

'This isn't mine,' he said.

The policeman said nothing. George looked round at the woman.

'This isn't mine.'

He smiled at the woman. She stared back at him, her face expressionless.

He took the photos out of the envelope. There were six photographs, postcard-sized. He looked at them one after the other. It took him a few moments to realize that what he was looking at was pornography.

The policeman was watching him.

'This isn't mine,' George said. 'This wasn't in here.'

The policeman still said nothing. George looked round at the woman again.

'This wasn't in here.'

The pictures were all much the same. It was pretty crude stuff. Black and white and over-exposed. A man and a woman on a bed, both naked except that the man was wearing socks.

There was something wrong with the woman. The man was normal but the woman looked deformed. Her head was too big for her body. She was half turned towards the man but her face was looking directly at the camera, as if her neck had been twisted round. Except that she didn't have a neck. There was just the face, balanced on the shoulders but disconnected, like a great white balloon.

It was a child's face, a little girl of four or five. She was smiling. He looked at the other photos. They were all the same. The woman was thin with small breasts, but it was obviously the body of a woman. A photo of a child's face had been superimposed. It was the most horrible thing he'd ever seen. It made him feel quite sick.

He stood up and pushed the photos away from him.

'For God's sake,' he said, 'you don't think this is mine?'

'Sit down, Mr Potter,' said the policeman.

'This is not mine. This wasn't in here. For God's sake.'

'Sit down, would you.'

George sat down.

'Now,' said the man, leaning forward and putting his elbows on the table, 'I want to make this very clear to you. Possession of this material is an offence. I'm sure you're aware of that. What we're interested in is the supplier. We want to know where you got it. If we get the name of the supplier, well, then we'll see. If we don't, then all we've got is you.'

'I don't believe this,' George said. This was a nightmare. He was going to wake up in a minute.

'What don't you believe?'

'Those are not mine.' The pictures were now lying on the table. The little girl's face smiled up at him.

'They were in your briefcase.'

'Then somebody put them there.'

'You're not suggesting we put them there?'

'I'm not suggesting anything,' George said. 'I'm saying those pictures are not mine. They weren't there before. Somebody put them there.'

'Why would anybody want to do that?'

'How the hell do I know? It was stolen, wasn't it? Somebody had it. Somebody put them there.'

'Thieves usually take things out,' the man said. 'They don't put them in.'

'You don't seriously think I'd walk around with that sort of stuff? I'm a schoolteacher.'

'Personally,' said the man, 'I think you're a piece of shit.'

The man took his elbows off the table and for a moment George thought he was going to hit him. What if he did? What if he punched him somewhere it didn't leave a mark? The man would deny it. The woman would deny it.

He heard the chair scrape behind him. The woman had stood up.

'Can I have a word, sir?' she said. It was the first time she'd spoken. She opened the door and went out of the room. The man got up from his chair and followed her.

'Don't go away, Mr Potter,' he said, and closed the door.

George was desperately trying to think what his rights were. He ought to know. He hadn't been charged. He hadn't been cautioned. Was he entitled to see a solicitor? Was he entitled to just walk out and go home? People like him knew these things. It was only stupid people who let

96

themselves get bullied like this. It didn't happen to middle-class people with an education. They stood up for themselves. They knew their rights.

The door opened and the man came back in. He stood and looked at George with a puzzled expression on his face, as if he'd never seen him before. He walked over to the table and picked up one of the sheets of paper from the briefcase.

'Weston Secondary,' he said. 'That's where you work, isn't it? Weston Secondary?'

'Yes. Look, I think I'd better see a solicitor before –'

'Is that the one near Weston Primary?'

'Just across the road.'

The man stared at George for a moment.

'Jesus,' he said.

11

'Now, look here,' George said when the new policeman came into the room, 'I want to get a few things straight here.'

The other one, the one with the shoulders who had called him a shit, had gone out of the room and George had been left on his own for twenty minutes and then the door opened and the new one came in. He was older, thinner. George started shouting at him.

'It's getting on for three bloody hours since I walked into a bloody police station to report a theft and since then I've been driven all over the town, I've had nothing to eat or drink, I'm cold and I'm hungry, I've been shown photos that are supposed to be mine that I've never seen before, I've been insulted, I haven't had a chance to make a phone call, nobody knows I'm here, I haven't seen a solicitor, and if you people don't start following a few rules around here I'm just getting up and I'm walking out.'

He took a deep breath and planted his feet firmly on the floor. He felt better. He was beginning to feel just a little bit more in control. The police had rules. They bent them, as everybody knew, but they had them, and they couldn't bend them too far. The trick was to behave as if he knew what the rules were. At least now they knew they weren't dealing with an idiot. They knew they were dealing with somebody who could stick up for himself.

The policeman leaned back against the wall and folded his arms.

'Fine,' he said.

'What?'

'Walk out if you like. I'm not stopping you.'

George needed a moment to take this in. The man was leaning casually against the wall. He had spoken quietly. He seemed very different from the one with the shoulders.

'I'm not under arrest?'

'Have you been told you're under arrest?'

'No.'

'Then you're not under arrest.'

This was too easy. It was a trick. It was the old hard cop, soft cop routine. George had seen the films. Unless they'd genuinely realized they'd made a mistake.

'What's your rank?' George said.

'Chief inspector,' the man said. 'My name is Rosewall.'

'And that other one? The one who was in here just now?'

'He's an inspector.'

'He called me a shit,' George said.

'Did he really?' The man sounded genuinely concerned. 'I'm terribly sorry about that, Mr Potter. You know how it is.' He nodded towards the envelope on the table. George had put the photos back inside. He couldn't bear to look at them. 'People tend to get a bit emotional about that sort of thing.'

'Yes, well, I suppose I can understand that.'

'If you want to make a complaint . . .'

'No, it doesn't matter.'

'That's very good of you.'

The man was still leaning against the wall with his arms folded. He was George's age at least, medium build but with a bit of a paunch, and totally unthreatening.

George was rooted to the spot. He'd worked himself up to have a row and demand his rights, and now this new man was being so nice to him he didn't know what to do.

'I'm free to go? Really?'

'That's what I said.'

'What about the photos?'

'You said they're not yours.'

'Yes, yes I did. They're not mine.'

'Well, then,' said the man, 'we can't charge you with anything if they're not yours.' He pushed himself away from the wall and walked over to the table. He picked up the envelope, pulled out one of the photos and looked at it briefly, then slipped it back inside. He dangled the envelope by the flap between his thumb and forefinger. 'Mind you,' he said, 'it's nasty stuff, this. Turns my stomach, to be quite honest.'

'Don't you think it turns mine?'

'It would be helpful,' said the man, 'if you could answer a few questions. Only take five minutes.'

'You said I was free to go.'

'So you are. If you don't like the questions, you don't answer them. If you want to get up and walk out, fair enough. Would be helpful, though. We don't really want this sort of stuff in circulation if we can help it, do we?' He gestured towards one of the chairs. 'Five minutes?'

George sat down. He was still suspicious. The man was being almost too nice, too reasonable, as if there were an edge of sarcasm to it.

'You said you were hungry. Would you like a sandwich?'

'No,' George said, 'if it's only five minutes.'

The man sat down opposite him.

'You see, I'm just trying to get the picture straight in my own mind,' he said. He picked up the envelope, took out the photos and spread them on the table like a hand of cards. George looked away. 'You've never seen these before today?'

'That's right.'

'So you've no idea where they might have come from. You couldn't give us any help with that?'

'No idea at all.'

'So what we have to assume is that somebody went to the trouble of breaking into your car and stealing a radio in order to put the photos in your briefcase. Would you agree?'

'I suppose so.'

'Why would they want to do that?'

'I don't know.'

'Well, what do you think? A joke?'

'Perhaps. Or perhaps they were trying to incriminate me, I don't know.'

'Trying to incriminate you,' said the man slowly, one syllable at a time, 'I see. So they put the photos in the briefcase on the off-chance that we might find it. Is that what you're saying?'

'I don't know,' George said. When he tried to explain it, he realized how unlikely it all sounded. 'All I know is I've never seen them before.'

'No,' said the man, 'so you said. Why would anyone want to incriminate you? Any ideas at all?'

'I don't know.'

'All a bit of a puzzle, isn't it, Mr Potter?' The policeman smiled. It was the first time his face had shown any expression at all. 'Photos in your briefcase that seem to have got there on their own. A robbery that might not have been a robbery. People trying to incriminate you for no reason. A bit of a puzzle.' He smiled again.

George couldn't argue with anything he'd said, but there was something in the man's voice, an exaggerated lilt in the intonation, that told him the man didn't believe a word he was saying.

'Yes, I suppose it is.'

'And you can't offer any sort of explanation for it?'

'No, not really.'

'Well, thank you for your help, Mr Potter.'

'Is that it?'

'Unless there's something else you want to say.'

George hesitated. Now that it was over, he almost didn't want to go. He hadn't explained himself properly. He hadn't been convincing. He wanted them to believe him. He wanted this man to believe him.

'Will you need to talk to me again?'

'I can't say at this stage.'

George stood up. He picked his briefcase up off the table.

'Can I take this?'

'It's your property.'

The policeman remained seated, watching George as he walked towards the door.

'We'll have to keep your photos, of course,' he said.

George froze for a moment, then went out without looking back.

It hadn't taken Rosewall long to decide that there was no point in charging Potter. The inspector who'd interviewed him, whose name was Adams, had been jumping up and down as if he'd just caught a murderer single-handed, but Rosewall had seen too many cases slip through his fingers to get excited about it at this stage. Incidentally, it had taken Adams rather a long time to admit that it was his sergeant who had actually made the connection between Potter and Daisy Beale's school. Adams was ambitious. Nothing wrong with ambition, but Rosewall believed in giving credit where it was due.

As far as the photos were concerned, if Potter swore blind he'd never seen them before his briefcase was stolen, there wasn't much of a case. And if they didn't have the supplier, the DPP probably wouldn't bother proceeding with it. Rosewall had thought for a moment that the face in the photographs might be Daisy's face, but it wasn't. It was just the face of a little girl, probably cut out of a magazine. He had seen photos like these before. They were cheaper to produce than the real thing and a lot safer for the supplier if he was caught. His lawyer would argue that the child wasn't really in the photo, and it was a devil of a job to establish what offence had actually been committed.

So what had they got, when it came down to it? Potter's school was opposite Weston Primary, attended by Daisy Beale. He had plenty of opportunity to watch the children coming in and out, plenty of opportunity to notice Daisy – which was not to say he had ever done so. He was also in possession of some kiddy porn. It was something, but it wasn't a lot. They didn't have a shred of positive evidence linking Potter to Daisy.

Rosewall could have held him for twenty-four hours without charge and tried to get a confession. Once he'd seen Potter, he'd realized there wasn't much chance of that. He could have got a twelve-hour extension, but that would just have taken them into the early hours of the morning and Mr Potter was entitled to his eight hours' sleep. They'd have ended up by letting him go anyway.

Rosewall needed to know who he was dealing with. Potter was an unknown quantity. He had no record of any kind. It was going to take time, but at least now they had a suspect. They knew where he lived and they knew where he worked. They could pick him up at any time. They couldn't afford to rush it and get it wrong. If Rosewall arrested Mr Potter, he would arrest him for murder and he would make it stick.

Norman had gone to Sefton Road with Val after school. She had invited him to come and have a coffee and a proper look at the house. She'd shown him round and now they were out in the garden. It was almost too dark to see anything but it was obvious even to Norman, who was no gardener, that it was uncared for.

'I'm no good at gardens,' Val said. 'My parents used to do all sorts with it but I can't be bothered.'

'I thought you were good at everything,' Norman said. 'That's what they all say at school.'

'Most things, I am,' she said. 'Anything round the house. Not gardens.'

She had put an overcoat on to come outside. There was a raw wind. In the house, she had changed into jeans and a shirt with the sleeves rolled up but, unfortunately, only one button undone at the neck. She had untied her hair and now the wind lifted a lock of hair and blew it across her face.

Something moved in the long grass under a tree. Norman wasn't sure at first whether it was just the wind, but then it moved again. He parted the grass with his foot and looked in. A pair of feral eyes looked back at him.

'You've got a cat.'

'She's a stray,' Val said. 'She's been there a week. She eats out of the dustbin. She's tried to get in the house a few times.'

'How do you know it's a she?'

'She's pregnant. Can't you see? When she's had her kittens she might go away.'

'What are you going to do with them?'

'Drown them,' she said.

'You could keep them.'

'There are enough cats in the world.'

'Take them to the vet.'

'It costs money. A bucket of water's cheaper and the end result's the same.'

'I suppose so.'

'Let's go inside,' she said. 'It's freezing out here and I can't light a cigarette in this wind.'

The whisky George poured himself when he finally got home that evening wasn't stiff, it was rigid. He'd really believed he was going to spend the night in a police cell. He found a packet of cook-from-frozen something or other in the freezer and stuck it in the oven.

He spent the rest of the evening sitting in his armchair with his whisky, staring in front of him, occasionally getting up to refill his glass. He must have eaten his dinner at some point because there was a dirty plate in the sink, but he couldn't remember what it was or what it tasted like.

He couldn't understand why they'd let him go. They obviously didn't believe a word he'd said about the photos. If it was an arrestable offence, which apparently it was, why hadn't they arrested him? The policeman who'd called him a shit had asked him about the primary school, where the little girl had gone. So why hadn't the other one, the chief inspector, asked him anything about it? None of it made any sense.

And how did the photos get in his briefcase in the first place? The only explanation was that somebody had faked the robbery on his car, planted the photos and then left the briefcase where it was bound to end up in the hands of the police. There was no other way to explain it. But it didn't sound any more convincing to him than it had done to the police. No wonder they didn't believe him.

Suppose he was right. Who would do something like that? Who hated him that much? He'd had rows with the Hodges. He'd had rows with a number of people at the school over the years. Just about everybody, in fact. It just didn't seem possible that anybody hated him enough to try to frame him as . . . as what? A paedophile? A murderer? Was that it? Were the police supposed to make the connection with the primary school? Was that part of the plan? It was all too horrible to think about, and if he went on like this he was going to become completely paranoid.

It was no use sitting here all night drinking himself stupid. He had a job to go to in the morning. He started getting ready for bed.

There was one good thing. The police didn't know about the stories the Pelham boy was telling. If they'd known about that, he would have been done for.

12

'Oh dear,' said Audrey Potter, when she had been assured that her ex-husband was not ill and had not been in an accident, 'what's he done now?'

'Why do you say "now"?' said Rosewall.

'Just an expression. What's he done?'

Twenty-four hours after he had walked into the police station, Potter remained an unknown quantity. They had been unable to find anything incriminating about him, or even anything mildly interesting. No record of any kind.

Twenty-nine years a teacher. Divorced, no children. Not a blemish on his character until he turned up with some dirty photos in his briefcase. Rosewall was trying to fill in the gaps.

First the wife, then the school. Then, when he was good and ready, Rosewall would talk to Mr Potter again.

If Potter, on the face of it, was an unlikely murderer, Mrs Potter was an even more unlikely murderer's wife. Women who lived with men like that were usually either as nasty as the men or they were soft in the head. She was neither.

She was the sort of woman who is described as handsome. Being fifty suited her. She was tall and slim with greying hair which she made no attempt to colour. Her make-up was discreet, her clothes expensive. She had the calm self-confidence which comes of a good family, a good education and a lifetime of taking for granted that one is liked and one's word is believed.

She was entirely unconcerned at having a policeman in the house. She offered him a chair, which he accepted, and a whisky, which he declined. She sat down on the sofa opposite him. She had a pair of spectacles hanging round her neck on a thin gold chain. She put them on from time to time ostensibly to get a better view of her visitor. Since she was probably long-sighted, he supposed this was meant to be intimidating. So it was. It was like being scrutinized by an aristocrat with a monocle.

'What do you think he might have done?' Rosewall said.

'Oh, I see,' she said, putting the glasses on. 'You don't tell me. I have to guess.'

'I'm sorry, but this might be quite a serious matter. I have to approach it in my own way. I'm not trying to trap you. I'm not trying to make you say anything you don't want to say.'

She gave him a look that told him he would have been wasting his time, and dropped the glasses.

'All right,' she said, 'I'll accept that, for the moment.'

He wondered if she had grown up with servants. He'd known people before who treated policemen this way, as the upper end of the servant class. What on earth had she been doing married to Potter?

Rosewall stood up and wandered across the room, looking at the pictures on the walls. His feet sank into the carpet, like walking on foam. The room was sparsely but tastefully furnished – a sofa, two deep armchairs, a coffee table, a huge sideboard. He was sure the taste was perfect. If he had tried to furnish a room that way, he would have got one thing glaringly wrong. He was sure that nothing in Mrs Potter's house was wrong.

'How would you describe your husband,' he said, 'in a word or two?'

'Bolshy.'

'Violent?'

'Good heavens, no. He wouldn't hurt a fly. George's battles are strictly verbal.'

'Does he have many battles?'

'Quite a few. He has strong opinions. He doesn't suffer fools gladly. Come to that, he doesn't suffer anybody gladly.'

'Battles at work?'

'Of course. He always had. He doesn't seem to have mellowed with age.'

'You've seen him recently?'

'He was here for dinner at the weekend.'

'May I ask what you talked about?'

'The school,' she said, 'what else? He always talks about the school. He thinks they're all out to get him.'

'Are they?'

'No, of course not. It's complete ballocks.'

Rosewall's expression gave nothing away, but he was shocked. He didn't expect ladies to use language. He was always careful not to use language himself in the presence of ladies, and he didn't expect them to use it. Scrubbers, yes. Ladies, no.

'Thank you for being so frank,' he said.

'I don't think I've said anything so far,' she said, putting the glasses on, 'which would cause him to come to the attention of the police.'

'Can we leave that for a moment? Do you happen to know his domestic arrangements?'

'We sold the old house,' she said. 'We both bought smaller ones.'

With your money, Rosewall thought. There was something about Mrs Potter that shouted family money at him. If he was right, at least it suggested an amicable divorce.

'That wasn't quite what I meant,' he said.

'Oh, I see.' She laughed. It was a loud ejaculation of a laugh. Again, to Rosewall's mind not quite ladylike. 'You mean does he have a girlfriend. What they call a partner nowadays. Not as far as I know. He's not easy to live with. But then, he'd probably say I'm not either.'

'Was the separation amicable?'

'Totally. We simply reached the stage where we had nothing left to say to each other. Now, as you say, I've been frank. Could we get to the point of this conversation?'

Rosewall came back and sat in his chair.

'Mr Potter's car was broken into,' he said.

'Oh, poor George.'

'The radio was stolen, and a briefcase with some school papers and a watch. He was most concerned about the watch.'

'I gave it to him,' she said. 'It's sweet of him to be concerned.'

'When we recovered the briefcase –'

'You recovered it? Isn't that unusual?'

'We do recover things occasionally,' he said.

'And fairly unusual, I would have thought, for a chief inspector to be investigating a theft?'

'When we recovered the briefcase,' Rosewall said, 'there was something in it that he says doesn't belong to him.'

'What?'

'Child pornography.'

She didn't say anything. Her face was inscrutable, but Rosewall felt as if he had just committed some unforgivable lapse of good taste, like hanging plaster ducks over the fireplace. She got up from the sofa. Rosewall stood up.

'Is he in custody?'

'No.'

'Why not? It's an offence, isn't it?'

'We're making further enquiries.'

'Into what?'

'A number of matters.'

She thought about this for a moment.

'Does he have a solicitor?' she said. 'No, of course he doesn't have a solicitor. He wouldn't have.'

'A solicitor would be appointed,' said Rosewall, 'if it came to that.'

'Can I arrange a solicitor for him? I know someone.'

You would, Rosewall thought.

'Yes, of course.'

'Then, if charges are likely to be brought, I don't think I should say anything more to you.'

She stood in the centre of the room, calm, assured, angry perhaps, but it hardly showed. He had been dismissed and she was waiting for him to go. She belonged in this room. It was a beautiful room and she complemented it perfectly. Rosewall felt as if he had brought something dirty and ugly into the room.

'Can I ask you one last question?' he said.

'You may ask,' she said, 'and I shall tell you. It's the most preposterous story I have ever heard in my life.'

'You believe he knew nothing about it?'

'Of course I believe it.'

Rosewall believed she believed it. He wished for her sake he could have believed she was right.

'If there's anybody there but him,' his mother said, 'anybody at all, you get back in the car. Do you hear me? Straight back in the car.'

'Yes,' Alex said.

Alex had got home from school and changed out of his uniform and his mother was taking him to meet his father.

'We'll check before you get out of the car,' she said. 'Check there's nobody else there.'

'Yes.'

'You check while I find somewhere to park.'

'Yes,' Alex said.

'I won't have it. If he brings her, I won't have it.'

It had been arranged that he would meet his father outside McDonald's and his father would buy him dinner and then take him to the cinema and then bring him home.

They got to the corner of the main street and drove slowly along it. Alex peered out of the car window.

'There he is. There he is. I can see him.'

His father was standing right outside McDonald's, looking up and down the street. Alex wound the window down and stuck his head out and waved.

'Is he alone?'

'Yes, yes, he's alone.'

'Are you sure?'

'Yes.'

His father had seen the car and was waving back.

'There's nowhere to park,' his mother said. 'There's no-bloody-where to park. You'll have to jump out.'

Alex jumped out, dodged between the parked cars and ran towards where his father was standing.

'Hello, Dad,' he said.

'Hello, Alex, how are you?'

He reached up to put his arm round his father's neck. His father stepped back and held out his hand.

'We don't do that now, do we, Alex? You're grown up now.'

Alex shook his father's hand.

'So, how's your mum been keeping?'

'Fine,' Alex said. 'Well, she's been a bit funny lately.'

'Bound to be, bound to be.'

'She nags me a bit.'

'Bound to. She doesn't mean it.'

Alex was having a beefburger and fries and a milk shake. His father was just having a burger. They were sitting at a table in the corner, looking out at the street. His father looked just the same as ever. He was wearing the suit he always wore to work. He was looking very smart. Alex had thought that, living in Gatehouse Road with a slag, he might have started looking a bit scruffy.

They chewed on their burgers and looked out of the window. Alex had been waiting for this moment, and now he wasn't sure what to say. He knew what he wanted to say. He'd thought about it a lot. He'd decided they probably wouldn't go to the cinema. He wasn't really bothered about seeing a film. There was so much to talk about. They might just sit and talk all evening about the things that mattered.

'How's school?'

'Fine.'

'Keeping your end up, are you?'

'Yes, Dad.'

He had also decided not to say anything about what was happening at school. It would take ages to explain, and there were more important things to talk about. There would be time to talk about school when his father was back home. He would tell him all about it then. He might even tell him the truth about Mr Potter.

'How's the computer?'

His father had bought him a computer for his last birthday.

'Fine.'

'Good. Get some use for it, do you?'

'Yes.'

'Good. Burger all right?'

'Yes, fine.'

His father had half finished his. He put it down on the table and pushed it away from him. He looked out of the window, turned and smiled at Alex, and looked out of the window again.

Alex knew everything he wanted to say. He had all his questions lined up. The difficulty was getting the first one out. His father didn't seem to know how to get started either. Alex took the bull by the horns.

'When are you coming home?' he said.

His father didn't say anything for a while. He just sat looking out of the window.

'Why do you ask that?'

This struck Alex as a silly question. It was what they were here to talk about, wasn't it?

'I want to know.'

His father turned towards him and put on the look that adults put on when they think you're trying to pull the wool over their eyes.

'Was it your idea to ask me that?'

'Yes.'

'Did she tell you to ask me that?' Another wool-over-the-eyes look. 'You can tell me, Alex.'

'No.'

'Are you sure?'

'Honest.' He took a bite out of his burger. 'When are you coming home, Dad?'

His father turned right round and faced him across the table. Now he was beginning to look angry. Alex had his teeth in his burger. He took it out of his mouth.

'Look, Alex,' his father said, 'I want you to understand something. If we're going to get together from time to time, and I hope we are, you know, I really hope we are, you mustn't come and say things she tells you to say.'

'I'm not,' Alex said. 'She didn't tell me to say anything.'

'You're sure about that?'

'I'm sure,' Alex said.

'That's all right, then.'

Alex ate some of his fries and had a drink and gave it a moment.

'Why are you living with that woman?' he said.

Now his father was looking really angry.

'I don't want to hear any of that, Alex,' he said. 'None of that. I won't hear it from her and I won't hear it from you. Do you understand?'

'Yes, Dad.'

His father picked up his burger again, took a bite and chewed slowly. He looked out of the window again and then turned back towards Alex.

'You're a good boy, Alex,' he said. 'I'm proud of you. I really am. We understand each other, don't we?'

'Yes.'

'We want to go on seeing each other, don't we?'

'Yes, Dad.'

'Then you mustn't come here saying things for her. I don't want any messages from her. Do you understand?'

'Yes.'

'Good. Now, we've got a whole evening together.' He pushed his chair back. 'Eat up or that film will be half over.'

*

Rosewall had phoned the school. Mr Prewitt had gone home. Rosewall said it was urgent, got the address from his secretary and called on him at home.

It took him ages to open the door. Rosewall introduced himself.

'It's not really convenient,' said Prewitt, holding the door ajar on a chain. 'Couldn't we talk at school tomorrow? My wife's an invalid.'

'Will I disturb her?'

'She's upstairs asleep.'

'In that case we'll talk very quietly.'

Prewitt reluctantly opened the door and let him in. They went through into the living-room and sat down. It was a very different room from Mrs Potter's. There was too much furniture for the size of the room and there were too many knick-knacks scattered about. It seemed fussy and cramped. Rosewall actually felt more comfortable in this sort of room. He had grown up in rooms like this. He knew where he was with Donald Prewitt.

Unlike Mrs Potter, the headmaster had the sort of attitude towards the police that Rosewall appreciated. He was thoroughly disconcerted to have a policeman in the house. But there was more to it than that. From the moment Rosewall said he wanted to talk about George Potter, his manner had been distinctly edgy. Rosewall had no intention of leaving until he had found out why.

'George? I don't believe I've seen him for a couple of days. Has anything happened?'

'Mr Potter is perfectly well, as far as I know.'

'Is anything the matter?'

'His car was broken into. We're making enquiries.'

'Oh, good heavens,' he said. His relief was obvious. So, what had he been expecting? 'It didn't happen at the school, I hope.'

'No, sir. At his home. It was yesterday. Some time in the early hours of the morning, most likely.'

'Oh, thank heavens. I mean, I thought . . . I wondered . . .'

The headmaster really was in a dreadful tizzy. This was all highly satisfactory.

'Wondered what, sir?'

'Well, I know he's been under a lot of stress recently.'

'Oh, why is that?'

The headmaster took a while to answer. It was dawning on him that he had said more than he'd needed to.

'We all have our ups and downs,' he said.

'I see.' What Rosewall saw was a man who was thoroughly rattled and possibly withholding evidence. He took out his notebook and a pen. This usually unsettled people, and he wanted Mr Prewitt as unsettled as possible. 'Would you say Mr Potter was a popular member of staff?'

'George is very respected. He's one of my most experienced teachers.'

'That wasn't quite what I asked you.'

'What's this got to do with his car?'

'We were just wondering if there might be a personal motive.'

'Oh, I see. Well, he's not always the easiest man to . . . people don't always see eye to eye.'

'Does he have enemies?'

'Enemies? No, I wouldn't say enemies.'

At that moment there was a furious banging on the ceiling from the floor above.

'I have to go up,' Prewitt said.

'Of course.'

The headmaster got up and went upstairs. Rosewall could hear footsteps across the ceiling and muffled voices. In a few minutes, he came down again.

'She's all right,' he said. 'She just wanted to know who you were.'

'Sorry I disturbed her.'

'Was there anything else?' Prewitt said, as if the conversation might have been drawing to its close.

'I was asking whether Mr Potter had enemies. What I was thinking was, is there anybody who dislikes him enough to play a practical joke on him? Let's say a rather elaborate and very nasty practical joke?'

'Joke? His car, you mean? No, good heavens, nothing like that.'

'What about the kids?'

'Kids? The pupils? No, I'm sure . . .'

'No history of that sort of thing?'

'We've had minor vandalism, of course. Graffiti and so on. Nothing like that. Going to a teacher's house and breaking into his car? No, I'm sure not.'

'Well,' said Rosewall, 'in that case . . .' He closed his notebook and stood up. The headmaster stood up. Once again, his relief was all too obvious. Whatever he was trying to hide, he thought he'd got away with it. 'I hope we haven't disturbed Mrs Prewitt too much.'

'No, not at all.'

They shook hands. Rosewall turned towards the door.

'Unless there's something else you'd like to tell me,' he said.

'I don't understand.'

'I'm afraid I wasn't entirely frank with you before, sir. This is actually a murder investigation.'

The headmaster slumped back into his chair.

'God bless us,' he said.

'I'm investigating the murder of Daisy Beale.'

'Oh, God bless us.'

'Now, sir, is there anything else you'd like to tell me?'

The headmaster looked up at him. He had turned terribly white.

'Well, there's the boy, of course. But I'm still looking into it. I can't . . . I have to think of the school.'

'Yes, sir.'

'I'm still looking into it.'

'No, sir,' said Rosewall, 'you were looking into it. Now I'm looking into it.' He opened his notebook again. 'Tell me about the boy.'

Rosewall made his third visit of the day, which he had not expected to make, to a house in Sefton Road only two doors away from the spot where Daisy Beale had disappeared. He couldn't interview the Pelham boy straight away because he was out with his father. While he was waiting for the boy to return, Rosewall had a most interesting conversation with the mother.

13

'They've got him,' said Dora Beale.

It had been on the radio. A man was helping the police with their enquiries.

'You know what that means,' she said. 'They've got the beast.'

'They phoned me when you were out,' Sarah said.

Dora almost screamed at her.

'Why didn't you tell me?'

'It might not be him. We won't know for a while.'

'It's him,' Dora said. 'I can feel it.'

After Daisy's funeral, the reporters had left Sarah alone. They had got as much out of the story as they could and they were waiting for an arrest.

For a time, she had been quite a celebrity. People who wrote newspaper columns and appeared on television programmes held strong opinions about her. Wherever the plight of the single-parent family was discussed, her name was mentioned. It was accepted as a matter of public record that Sarah had neglected Daisy, shutting her out of the house and leaving her to roam the streets in order that she might entertain her boyfriends. Defenders of the family denounced her. Others upheld her right to be promiscuous if she wished.

With the discovery of the body, the focus of attention had moved away from her. There were a number of articles in the papers about the psychology of child abusers and then the story had petered out until it would be revived by the news of an arrest.

Sarah became obsessed with knowing how much Daisy had suffered and for how long. The police said that she had died within twenty-four hours of her disappearance. What had happened in those twenty-four hours? Sarah had not been told all the details of the state in which Daisy's body had been found, but she knew that she had been abused.

'They'll make him tell us?' she kept saying. 'They'll make him tell us what he did?'

'Of course they will,' said Dora.

'I have to know what he did. I have to know what she went through.'

'If they don't make him tell us,' Dora said, 'I will.'

It was Friday, two days after George had innocently walked into a police station to report that his car had been broken into. Now he was back at the station and this time he was under arrest. They had picked him up at home at eight o'clock in the morning while he was getting ready for school. They had bundled him into a car and driven him to the police station. He had entered the station with a policeman's jacket over his head.

'It's for your own protection,' one of them said. 'The press have got wind of this.'

He was brought before a sergeant in uniform and told to empty his pockets. A list was made of his possessions and then they were returned to him. He was informed of his right to a phone call and to legal advice. He had other rights, but he had forgotten what they were even before the sergeant had finished speaking. He was given various pieces of paper. He was given something called a custody record to sign to say that he had been informed of his rights and had understood them.

For the sergeant, this was obviously a routine which he had carried out again and again, day after day. His voice was flat, expressionless, almost mechanical. He spoke as if George perhaps might have been a little retarded. The words he was using were the words he always used, without variation. For him, this was an everyday occurrence.

For George, it was not. He had never been arrested before. It was all new and he was only taking in half of what was being said to him. What could they do to him? There were rules, he kept telling himself, there were rules. They had to do it by the rules. What it reminded him of was the induction of new pupils into the school. There they stood, silent and bewildered, while some condescending adult quoted rules at them which he understood and they didn't. On many occasions, the condescending adult in question had been George.

He used his phone call to ring Audrey. He didn't know who else to phone. When he told her he'd been arrested, she didn't sound surprised.

'I phoned Barrington yesterday,' she said, 'after that policeman was here. You remember Jack Barrington.'

'What policeman?'

'Never mind that,' she said. 'I'll phone him now as soon as the office opens. Tell them you've got a solicitor coming. Don't let them question you until he gets there.'

George was put in a cell to wait for his solicitor. People looked in at him through the window in the door from time to time. He could only see their eyes. He sat on the bed and read the bits of paper the sergeant had given him. In addition to his phone call and his legal advice, he was entitled to reasonable physical comfort, food and drink and access to a toilet. There was also a copy of the caution. This was reassuring. There were rules.

So what about all the people who had gone to prison for crimes they knew nothing about? There had been rules for them too.

It was over an hour before Barrington appeared. George was beginning to think he wasn't coming. He was a large red-faced man with polished grey hair and a bow tie. He came bustling into the cell like one of those doctors who believe in keeping the patient cheerful at all costs.

'Well, well, this is a bit of a pickle,' he said. 'Dirty photos, is it? Oh, dear me.' He sat down on the bed beside George.

George knew Barrington of old. He was a friend of Audrey's parents and he had acted for her in the divorce. He was typical of those members of Audrey's circle whom George had spent his married life avoiding. He had always had a way of treating George as if he were a persistent offender whose circumstances were well known to the legal profession, but George was relieved that he was there. Here was somebody who was at least supposed to be on his side.

George told him about the theft from his car and the briefcase and the photos.

'Protection of Children Act,' said Barrington, '1978. Very unpleasant. Stick to your story.'

'It happens to be true,' George said.

'Jolly good.'

'And there's something about my school being opposite the primary, where that little girl went. The Daisy girl. They asked me about it before.'

Barrington's attitude changed. He made himself more comfortable on the bed and looked at George with a new interest, almost a new respect, as if a murderer might be worth dragging himself out of the office for.

'What's your connection with that?'

'None at all. My school's opposite the primary, that's all.'

'So what the devil are they playing at?'

'I think there might be something else,' George said. He'd guessed why they'd brought him in. It only made sense if they knew something they hadn't known two days before. There was only one thing it could be. He told Barrington about the Pelham boy.

The solicitor had started making notes on the back of an envelope. He looked at George from time to time but his expression gave nothing away. The jollity had gone, though.

'We have to assume they know about that, then,' he said, putting the envelope in his pocket and standing up. 'All right, just answer their questions unless I tell you not to. Don't tell them any lies but don't volunteer anything they don't ask. And don't tell them anything you haven't told me. I hate surprises.'

Barrington was sitting beside George, but at an angle so that they had easy eye-contact. The first thing he had done was to move his chair from where the police had put it. Sitting on the opposite side of the table were the chief inspector from two days ago and George's old friend with the barn-door shoulders.

The interview was being recorded. The chief inspector had produced two tapes in their wrappers, unwrapped them in front of George and placed them in a twin-deck machine. He explained that one of the tapes, the master, would be sealed in George's presence when the interview was over. The other tape was the working copy. When the recorder had been switched on, he identified those present. DCI Rosewall, DI Adams, Mr Potter, Mr Barrington. The caution which George had been given at the time of his arrest was repeated.

Rosewall was being brisk and businesslike. It was impossible to tell how much he knew or what he believed. Adams was glowering at George across the table but was keeping his mouth shut.

They began with the photographs and went over the same ground they had covered two days before.

'You still maintain,' said Rosewall, 'that you have never seen those photographs before?'

'No.'

'You have no idea how they came to be in your briefcase?'

'No.'

'The briefcase was out of my client's possession for nearly twelve hours,' said Barrington. 'I understand it had been forced open. He can't be held responsible for anything that was found in it.'

'Let Mr Potter answer the questions, would you, sir?' said Rosewall. He turned to George. 'Why didn't you report the briefcase as missing?'

'I did.'

'No, Mr Potter, you didn't.' Rosewall looked at a sheet of paper in front of him. 'You reported a radio and a watch.'

George had forgotten about that. Of course it looked suspicious now.

'I wasn't bothered about the briefcase. It was an old one. I just wanted the watch back.'

'I see. So, you reported the theft of the radio and the watch but you didn't bother mentioning the briefcase even though it was stolen. Why was that?'

'I've just told you. I wasn't bothered about it. Look, if I'd known about the photos, I wouldn't have reported the theft at all, would I?'

Rosewall ignored this and pushed the sheet of paper to one side.

'Do you know an Alexander Pelham?'

This was it. They knew. George's heart sank.

'Yes. He's in the second year at my school.'

'Do you know him?'

'Slightly. I've spoken to him once, I think.'

'Would you cast your mind back to Tuesday and Wednesday of last week.' Rosewall gave him time to cast his mind back. 'Tell me what happened.'

George told him what had happened. He had seen young Pelham in a classroom on the Wednesday afternoon at about four o'clock. He had not seen him on the Tuesday nor on the Wednesday morning. He had not at any time offered him a lift in his car.

'I'm told he wasn't in school on the Wednesday,' said Rosewall. 'Nobody seems to have seen him but you.'

'I saw him,' George said.

'So the boy is lying?'

'Yes.'

'He made it all up out of the blue?'

'Yes.'

'Why would he do that?'

'I don't know. He had a day off school. He had to come up with some sort of an excuse.'

'A day off school,' said Rosewall, 'yes, of course. That would be the day you saw him in the classroom?'

'Yes.'

'The day he wasn't there?'

123

'He was there at four o'clock.'

'All right,' said Rosewall, 'let's leave that for the moment. Why should he accuse you? Why you in particular? You say you hardly know him.'

'I don't know.'

'It all gets more and more mysterious, doesn't it, Mr Potter?' There was that lilt in the voice again that he remembered from their last meeting – the one that said, I don't believe a word you're saying.

George said nothing. He was beginning to get sick of this, and he was beginning to get angry. He realized that, suddenly, he wasn't frightened any more. He had been stupid. They had no evidence against him. They couldn't possibly have any evidence because he didn't know anything about the photos or about the Pelham boy and there couldn't be evidence of things he'd never done. They were fishing, trying to intimidate him, hoping he would make a mistake, hoping he would give them something. They were playing games with him.

'So, you never asked him to get into your car?' Rosewall was saying.

'No.'

'You refute the whole incident?'

'I don't refute it,' George said testily. 'I deny it. If I refute it, it means I provide a counter-argument.'

Barrington looked across at him, half closed his eyes and shook his head to say no.

'Very well,' said Rosewall, 'you deny it?'

'Yes.'

'It's my client's word against the boy's,' Barrington said wearily, 'unless you have witnesses. That's all there is to it.'

'Do you know Daisy Beale?'

George had been waiting for this.

'No,' he said. 'Only what I've read in the papers.'

'Do you remember where you were on the morning of Saturday –'

'At home,' George said. 'I'm always at home on a Saturday morning. Usually in bed.'

'Alone?'

'Yes.'

'Might I ask,' said Barrington, 'how many charges you're contemplating against my client, if any? We seem to be on to number three.'

'Just a few more questions,' said Rosewall.

'Shouldn't you make up your bloody mind,' George said, 'what it is I'm supposed to like? I mean, do I like little girls or do I like twelve-year-old boys?'

'Why don't you tell us what you like,' said Adams. It was the first time he'd spoken.

'Don't answer that,' said Barrington.

'It's a fair question,' Rosewall said. 'You've been divorced two years. You live alone. What are we talking about here? Girlfriends? Boyfriends? Looking at dirty pictures and making your own arrangements?'

'Don't answer.'

'I wasn't going to.'

'Would you consent to giving an intimate sample?'

'What?' George didn't know what he was talking about. What sample? He opened his mouth to answer.

'No,' Barrington said, 'he wouldn't. Don't pull a trick like that. You have no authorization. You have no reasonable grounds.'

'What's going on?' George said.

'I'd like to speak to my client alone,' said Barrington. 'It's time we had a break, anyway.'

'It's in his best interests,' said Rosewall. 'Tell him that.' He stood up. 'Interview suspended . . .'

'What's going on?' George said, when they were alone. 'What's an intimate sample?'

'Blood,' said Barrington. 'It's the Daisy Beale murder. They presumably know the killer's blood group. It's never been made public, but it's not surprising if she was abused.'

George didn't know whether to laugh or cry. It had been a nightmare and now suddenly it was a farce.

'Are you telling me,' he said, 'they could have eliminated me the moment I walked in here? All I had to do was give blood? I've been through all this and they could just have given me a blood test?'

'Calm down,' Barrington said. 'It's not as easy as that. In the first place, you'd only be in the clear if your blood doesn't match their sample. And there are still the other matters.'

'What should I do?'

'It's up to you. My reading of it is that it's the murder of the little girl they're really concerned about. They're under a lot of pressure and you're the nearest thing to a suspect they've got. If your blood type doesn't match, you're in the clear. They could still proceed on the other matters, of course, but it's all pretty flimsy. They've no corroborating evidence. Unless you're silly enough to confess to something, my guess is you'd walk out of here. On the other hand, if your blood does match, we say it's a coincidence, but . . .'

'What would they do?'

'They could get an extension and go on questioning you. We'd oppose it. Or they might decide it's worth charging you and then looking for more evidence. They'll search your house, search your car, talk to everybody who knows you. They'll turn your whole life over. You'll be famous.'

'What do you advise?'

'Do you know your blood group?'

'No.'

'If it's a common one,' Barrington said, 'you'd be taking quite a risk.'

14

The next day the newspapers reported that the police, having arrested a sex beast, had been obliged to release him for lack of evidence. The beast in question, who could not be named, was now free and roaming the streets as if butter wouldn't melt in his mouth.

'I couldn't believe it when they told me he'd been arrested,' said Don Prewitt. 'We've never had anything like that at the school.' He seemed to be having difficulty getting comfortable in his armchair. 'And then the next thing I knew, he was out.' He had a sip of his drink. 'I phoned the chief inspector this afternoon. We had quite a long talk. I mean, I had to know what the situation was, for the sake of the school. He quite understood. He was very sympathetic.'

'You had no choice,' said Pris.

'Absolutely no choice,' said Derek.

'He's in the clear as far as the little girl is concerned,' said Don. 'Wrong blood group, apparently. As for the other business . . .'

'He's still a paedophile,' said Pris. 'From what you've said about the boy, there doesn't seem much doubt.'

'No doubt at all,' said Derek.

The Hodges had invited the headmaster for dinner. It had been a spur-of-the-moment invitation, though they had only been saying just the other day how long it was since they'd had him round. After the preliminary enquiries about Sally – she was feeling more cheerful at the moment – George had been the sole topic of conversation.

In spite of the short notice, Don had been able to leave Sally for an hour or two, and Pris had managed to get the dinner sufficiently under control that they had twenty minutes to sit and have a pre-dinner drink.

'I'm sure the Pelham boy's telling the truth,' said Don. 'The police think so too. I do see their point of view, though. Putting a twelve-year-old in court. It's not ideal. The mother's against it.'

'I can't believe there were no witnesses,' said Derek. 'Right in front of the school, four o'clock in the afternoon.' He walked over to Don's chair and topped up his glass.

'Thank you,' said Don. 'And there are problems about the photos. They're not taking any action over that either.'

'What photos?' said Pris.

'Oh dear,' said Don, 'I wasn't supposed to say anything about that. He thought I ought to know, for the sake of the school, but as they're not proceeding . . . This is all in the strictest confidence, Pris. I shouldn't have told you about the Pelham boy, except . . .'

'What photos, Don?'

'Oh well, I suppose it'll come out. He had photographs of children on him. Disgusting stuff. I can't believe it.'

'That's interesting,' said Pris. She sat back in her chair and rocked her glass gently in both hands, watching the wine lapping in the bottom. 'I wouldn't have expected that. I'd have said it was pretty well repressed. Came to the surface when he was under stress. It's often the case. It's well documented.' She looked up suddenly. 'If he was a pornography user, that's different. He knew what he was.'

'Why do you think he became a teacher, darling? He always said he hated the job. You know the way he talked. It's obvious when you think about it.' Derek got up and walked over to Don's chair and offered a peanut. Don declined. Derek popped a handful in his mouth.

'He can never set foot in a school again,' said Pris. 'You do realize that, Don?'

'Let him try,' said Derek, munching peanuts.

'You have to go to the governors, Don. It has to be done and it has to be done quickly.'

'It might be difficult, Pris. He hasn't been charged with anything. I don't know how the police could ignore the photos, but apparently they have. Whatever we may think of him, strictly speaking he's an innocent man.'

'You're talking about the evidence needed for a conviction,' she said. 'I'm talking about the evidence needed to keep him out of school. Call it early retirement, call it indefinite sick leave, call it whatever you want. We owe it to the children. They're our first responsibility.'

'They certainly are,' said Derek.

'The governors will follow your lead, Don. Leave the county to me.'

'It's terribly difficult, Pris. I suppose it will all have to come out sooner or later. The photos and everything. The Pelham boy. It's the school I worry about.'

'People have a right to know who they're working with,' said Derek. 'The parents have a right to know.'

'How would you feel if he did it again?' said Pris. 'If he went further next time?'

'You're right, of course,' said Don. 'One wants to be fair and everything, but as far as the police are concerned he's a paedophile. That ought to be good enough for me.'

'I can't believe he'd dare show his face,' said Derek, helping himself to another handful of peanuts. 'If I have anything to do with it, I can promise you the whole school will know what he is.'

'Sounds like a frame-up to me,' said Sandra.

'Why?' said Rosewall. Without mentioning any names, he had been telling his daughter as much as he could about the progress of the Daisy Beale investigation, trying to get her curious about his work. She had actually shown a spark of interest in the case. She had described it as sick. This was the strongest term of condemnation she knew. Sick was worse than gross.

'It's all a bit neat,' she said. 'It's like those detective stories, you know, where all the clues pile up and they all point to the wrong person. And the police are so thick they believe it.'

'In my experience,' said Rosewall, ignoring the slur on his profession, 'when the clues all point to the same person, they point to the right person.'

'That's what I said. The police always get it wrong.'

'Anyway,' he said, 'the person in question is no longer a suspect, not for the murder, at least. He's just a rather dirty little man.'

'Maybe not even that,' she said. 'If you know who did it half-way through, Dad, you don't know who did it.'

'In real life,' said Rosewall, 'you never know when you're half-way through.'

'I'll bet you,' she said. 'If it turns out he didn't do any of it, you owe me a hundred pounds.'

'You haven't got a hundred pounds to bet, Sandy.'

'Not that sort of bet,' she said. 'I said you'd owe me, not I'd owe you. You never listen.'

'Make it ten,' said Rosewall.

'There's no smoke without fire,' said Dora Beale. 'That's all I can say.'

'It wasn't him,' said Sarah. 'They said it wasn't him. They did a blood test.'

'They can get them wrong. They get things wrong all the time. Look at your father's legs. Three doctors, including that black one. They all got it wrong.'

130

'Oh, shut up about his bloody legs,' Sarah said. 'If you're bothered about him, go home.'

'I won't go home till he's caught,' Dora said. 'I swore that when I came. I won't go till I've looked him in the face.'

Sarah had been trying to persuade her mother to go home for some time. She couldn't stand having her round the house any more. She just talked about Daisy all the time, what an angel she'd been, how there would never be another like her. It was driving Sarah mad.

The fact was that she couldn't stand her mother. In the first weeks after the murder, when there had been the phone calls and all those horrible things in the newspapers, it had been a comfort to have someone in the house, anyone. Now she couldn't stand it.

She had decided some time ago that she would go back to work, but she hadn't said anything to Dora yet. They desperately needed the money, but that wasn't the real reason. The most important thing was that it would give her something to do that would fill a few hours of the day. That was all there was to do until he was caught, just fill the time.

Then there would be the ordeal of the trial. She knew how horrible it would be, how it would bring everything back, but she knew she would have to sit through every minute of it. She owed it to Daisy to hear every word that was said. But it might be months before there was a trial, even years. She couldn't just sit around the house and wait, listening to Dora. She would go mad.

When it was finally over and he was caught and convicted and she knew everything that had happened, she could begin to make her peace with Daisy. She would go to the grave, ask Daisy's forgiveness for leaving her to walk down the lane alone, perhaps receive it, perhaps even forgive herself. Until then, it was just a question of getting through the day. A few hours at the school would help. She'd have people to talk to, somebody to talk to besides her mother.

'I'm going back to work,' she said. 'I'm going back to the school on Monday.'

'You never are,' Dora said.

'It'll do me good. It'll take my mind off things.'

'Are you sure you're ready?'

'Of course I am,' she said. 'It'll be nice to see everybody again. It'll be nice to hear the gossip.'

15

When George left the police station, he'd thought that things couldn't possibly get any worse. In the next few days, they did. Over the weekend, he saw a colleague in the street and the man had walked past without speaking, without looking at him except for one moment when their eyes met and George could see the anger and the embarrassment. The new week began with a letter telling him he was suspended from the school. They knew. Everybody knew. They knew it and they believed it.

After that, he didn't go out for a couple of days. He just sat at home testing the theory that the best way to drink is little and often. The phone kept ringing. He was pretty sure it was Audrey. He desperately wanted to talk to someone – preferably someone who didn't think he was a child molester, if such a person could be found – but he was afraid to answer in case it wasn't her.

Eventually, he pulled himself together and went to see her on the pretext of saying thank you for the solicitor. When he was standing outside her door, he was almost afraid to ring the bell. If she believed it too, it was the end.

He needn't have worried. She put her arms round him and kissed him and then started talking and she hadn't finished yet. It was like being married again.

'So that's settled,' she said, when she finally paused for a breath. They were sitting in the living-room and George was wondering whether there was a drink in the house. 'You're going to stop feeling sorry for yourself.'

He had no intention of doing anything of the kind.

'I've got bloody good reason to feel sorry for myself. I've told you what the police said. They believe the boy. They believe the photos were mine. They've got me in the computer as prime suspect for any offence against a child from now till Doomsday. I'm suspended from the school. I'll never work again. Everybody's treating me like a leper. It's even in the papers. Have you seen the papers? I'll have my picture on the front page next. If you see this man, kick his teeth in.'

'Have you finished?' she said.

'I told you they were out to get me. Did you believe me? No. Ballocks, you said. I distinctly remember that. We were in the middle of dinner. They're out to get me, I said. Ballocks, you said.'

'All right, don't go on about it. So I was wrong about that.'

'I can't believe this is happening to me.'

'It's not happening,' she said. 'It's being done. That's the first thing to get straight. Somebody is doing this to you.'

'It's happening, it's being done. What difference does it make?'

'A lot,' she said. 'Come through into the kitchen. I'll make you a sandwich. You don't look as if you've had anything recently that didn't come out of a bottle. You stink like a brewery.'

She got up and went into the kitchen. George followed. It always felt strange being in this house. The furniture was the stuff they had had in the old house when they were together, the pictures were from the old house,

133

but everything was in the wrong place in the wrong rooms.

She took a piece of ham out of the fridge, cut slices off it and made him two thick sandwiches. He stood in the doorway and watched her. It really was like being married again. The house was wrong but she was the same. He should have known she wouldn't doubt him.

He was standing just behind her and he could have reached out and put his arms round her. He might have done if she hadn't moved at that moment. She went to a cupboard and took out a bottle of Scotch. She poured a small whisky and topped it up with rather more water than he would have given himself.

'Don't guzzle it,' she said, handing him the glass and a plate. 'You're not getting another one.'

George took his whisky and sandwiches and they went back into the living-room and sat down.

'So somebody is doing it to me,' he said. 'Why?'

'You were convenient, I should think.' She had put her glasses on to make the sandwiches. She hooked them off and let them fall on to the chain around her neck. 'The police must be desperate for an arrest. The whole country's up in arms about that little girl. They have to get a conviction and they have to get one soon. They're never going to let it rest. They needed a suspect, so somebody decided to give them one.'

He had been thinking about this. The more he thought about it, the less sense it made.

'What you're talking about,' he said, taking a bite of his sandwich, 'is some sort of conspiracy. It can't just be one person. The break-in, the photos . . . the Pelham boy would have to be part of it. Why me? I'm not worth the trouble.'

'Try thinking of it the other way round. It starts with the boy.'

'I don't know what that means,' he said, 'and I'm too tired to work it out.' He had a gulp of his whisky. He seemed to be half-way through it already.

'All right,' she said. 'I'll do the thinking. You can do the leg work.'

'Forget it. Thanks all the same, but forget it.'

'Oh, come on,' she said. 'You can't just take this lying down. Do you want everybody to think you're a criminal for the rest of your life?'

'At the moment, I don't bloody care.'

'Of course you do. Oh, I know it seems hopeless, darling, but look at it this way. One person knows the whole truth. One person knows you're innocent. We just have to find that person and wring it out of him.'

'How are you going to do that?' he said. 'Nag him to death?'

'God, that's typical of you. Stubborn as a pig, then one mishap and you roll over and die.'

'Mishap?' A mouthful of whisky went down the wrong way and it took him a while to stop coughing and spluttering. 'Is that what you call it?'

'Look at it from my point of view,' she said. 'I don't want the whole world thinking I spent twenty years married to a pervert.'

'I'm sorry,' he said. He was being horrible to her, and she was the only person who was prepared to believe in him. 'All right, supposing we do something. Where would we start?'

'There are two obvious places to start. One is the boy.'

'No,' he said, 'I can't go near the boy. The police were very clear about that. If I approach the boy, if I approach the mother, if I so much as set foot in the street –'

'If you can't,' she said, 'maybe I can. The other place to start is the briefcase. That can be your job. It didn't fall into the hands of the police out of the blue. Somebody gave it to them. Somebody went to a lot of trouble.'

'It was found at the railway station and handed in. Anybody could have put it there.'

'You don't get the idea, do you?' she said. 'We agree the boy isn't part of it. That would be preposterous. Do we agree? Yes. OK, so for some reason he starts making up stories about you. Then somebody decides to frame you. Why you? I'll tell you why. Because you're vulnerable. Somebody knows what stories the boy is telling. The photos were meant to back up what the boy was saying. Don't you see? That means it's somebody close to the Pelham family or close to the school. It's probably someone you know.'

'You mean somebody who's trying to get me out of the school?'

'Oh, for heaven's sake,' she said, 'I mean somebody who killed Daisy Beale. That's what this is all about. You were being framed for murder.'

'Why? Why frame anybody at all? Why go to all the trouble?'

'Something must have happened,' she said. 'Something happened to frighten him, put him under pressure. Did anything happen at the school?'

'No.'

'Nothing out of the ordinary, just before this briefcase business started?'

'No, nothing. Well, there was the staff meeting. Don said the police were coming back. They were going to interview us all again. It was just routine, though.'

'That fits,' she said. 'It was enough to frighten him. Somebody can't risk being interviewed too often.'

'No,' he said, 'I don't believe it. People who do things like that to children are simple-minded. They're totally inadequate. They've got a history of that sort of thing. You can see them coming a mile away. I don't know anybody like that.'

'So how do you explain it? Coincidence?'

'I don't know.'

'No, my darling,' she said, 'there's no coincidence. A disturbed little boy starts making up stories. Then the police are handed evidence to back up the stories. And it just so happens that you work across the road from Daisy Beale's school. If it hadn't been for the blood – and that wasn't public knowledge, was it? – you'd still be under arrest and facing charges. Somebody is doing this to you, somebody close to you, and he isn't simple-minded. He's clever and ruthless.'

'I don't know anybody who's clever and ruthless.'

'You wouldn't know if you did. Anybody who can do this is a psychopath.'

'Children aren't murdered by psychopaths,' George said. 'They're murdered by pathetic, inadequate misfits with a psychiatric record as long as your arm. Nobody like that would ever get near a school.'

'Somebody's got near,' she said. 'Somebody's got near to you.'

'Don't stand between her and the door,' Val said. 'She won't come in if you're in the way. She doesn't know you.'

Norman walked slowly across and stood beside the garden wall. The cat was sitting at the edge of the grass, watching them. Val had opened a tin of tuna and put some on a saucer. She put the saucer down in the doorway and backed away into the kitchen. She had already closed the door between the kitchen and the rest of the house.

'Come on, cat,' she said. 'Food.'

The cat sat and watched Val, occasionally turning her head to look at Norman. She seemed unconcerned by their presence, though she was a sufficient distance away that if either of them had moved towards her she could have been gone.

'Come on, you stupid cat,' said Val. 'You've tried to get into the house often enough.'

That was as may be. It was one thing to try to get into the house when she was not allowed to. It was quite another to be invited in and offered food when she had never been shown any such consideration before. The cat did not move.

'Shall I try to shoo her in?'

'Don't you do anything,' Val said. 'She'll be gone.'

Norman had managed to get away from school early and he knew Val had a free afternoon so he had come round to Sefton Road. The cat had had her litter. There were three kittens, three balls of fur with closed eyes and open mouths, under a tree at the bottom of the garden. Norman and Val had gone down to look at them and then they had been sitting in the kitchen, talking about all the gossip about George, when they saw the mother cat coming up the garden.

'Mmm,' said Val, picking up the saucer, 'delicious.' She put it down on the step outside the back door.

The cat began to move forward slowly, with her ears pricked up and her belly almost touching the ground. When she came level with where Norman was, she stood for a moment with one front paw raised and then she moved forward again. Val picked up the saucer and put it down just inside the kitchen door. The cat stopped again for a moment with one paw on the step and then crept into the doorway.

Once she had tasted the food, she was lost. Val allowed her one mouthful, then moved the saucer into the middle of the kitchen floor. The cat followed without raising her head, following the scent of the food. Val snatched her cigarettes and lighter off the table, then circled around behind her and closed the door, shutting her in.

'Right,' she said. 'Kittens.'

They went down the garden and fetched the kittens out from under the tree. Val brought two of them, holding them by the scruff of the neck. Norman brought the third. It was no bigger than the palm of his hand. Val put her two kittens down outside the back door and began filling a bucket from the garden tap. Norman was still holding his kitten.

He held it up in one hand with his fingers around its chest and looked at it. It wasn't a very attractive creature. Its eyes were shut and its legs were flailing as it tried to get free. Its fur was spiky and a little slimy, probably from the wet grass. It seemed an elemental sort of thing, just a heartbeat wrapped in wet fur.

Val had brought a piece of sacking up from the garden shed. She spread it on the ground and put her two kittens in the middle. They tumbled blindly over each other.

'Give that one here,' she said. When he didn't hand it over straight away, she looked up at him. 'Unless you want to keep it.'

Norman held the kitten up and looked at it again. He realized that what he possessed at that moment was nothing less than the power of life and death. There was no reason he shouldn't keep the kitten, take it home, give it its life. He had never had this sort of power before. He had never had any kind of power. Other people had power over him, the power to humiliate him, torment him. Women. The kids at the school.

The kitten was struggling quite violently now, but that only made it seem all the more vulnerable. The animal didn't know what was happening to it. He did. His was the power. It was his decision. Life or death. Thumbs up, thumbs down. He held the kitten tightly in his hand, feeling the heartbeat, prolonging the moment.

'Well?' Val said.

He handed her the kitten. She put it with the other two inside the sacking, pulled the corners together to fold it loosely into a bag and tied a piece of string around the neck. She took her jacket off and gave it to Norman.

'Hold this, will you,' she said. 'I don't want to get it wet.' She was wearing a short-sleeved blouse with a rather interesting neckline.

She lifted the bag, plunged it into the water and held it down, bending over the bucket. Norman stood and watched her. It wasn't entirely true that she had no breasts. She held the bag under for a couple of minutes, then released it and it rose to the surface of the bucket.

'That should do it.'

There was no movement from inside the bag. There were tiny drops of water glistening all along the backs of her hands and her arms. She straightened herself, lifted the bag out of the bucket and put it on the ground. Norman was still watching her.

'What are you looking at me like that for?' she said.

If he had the power of life and death, he had the power to do anything. There was no reason why he shouldn't do whatever he liked, take whatever he wanted. In the moment that he had held the kitten in his hand and then sent it to its death, he had felt not only the power but a kind of excitement that he might never feel again. He grabbed Val by the arm and pulled her towards him. He kissed her hard on the mouth and then let her go.

She looked at him for a moment, then went over to where she had left her cigarettes and lighter and picked them up.

'Next time,' she said, 'you could try asking.'

'You've got to tell him,' his mother said. 'I can't believe you didn't tell him last time.'

She had been on about it all evening. It was almost a week since Alex had seen his father, and he was due to see him again after school tomorrow. She'd questioned him about every word they'd said, over and over again, and she'd nagged him a lot because he hadn't told his father about Mr Potter.

'Tell him what you told that policeman,' she said. 'He's still your father, Alex. He's got rights, you know.'

This was news. He hadn't heard much about his father's rights before.

'I'll see if it comes up.'

'It's not a question of whether it comes up, Alex. You've told Mr Prewitt. You've told that policeman. You've told me. I don't see the harm in telling your own father.'

'All right, I'll tell him,' Alex said.

He knew what she was up to. He knew what her plan was. He would tell his father that one of the teachers had tried to get him into his car, that he had been afraid to go to school, that the police had been round, that Mr Potter wasn't allowed in the school any more. And what would his father do? He'd feel guilty because he hadn't been at home while all this was going on and he'd come rushing back. That was the plan. She thought he wasn't capable of working this out.

The problem was that Alex didn't know whether he wanted his father back any more. He'd been thinking about this. If he came back, what would happen? It might be all right for a while, then they'd start fighting again. Perhaps his father would go back to the slag. Perhaps there would be another slag. Maybe things were better as they were.

'You must tell him, Alex. I mean it. If you don't, I will.'

He didn't believe this. She'd sworn often enough she'd never speak to his father again as long as he was living with the slag.

'I'll tell him, Mum,' he said. 'I'll tell him.'

16

The day after he had been to see Audrey, George was in the office of the transport police at the railway station. This did not strike him as a good place to be – he was allergic to policemen at the moment – but Audrey had insisted. She would investigate the Pelham family while George followed the trail of the briefcase.

He slunk in and approached the policeman at the desk, looking, he was sure, the very picture of a child molester. He explained his business.

'Briefcase?' the man said, glancing up. 'Never heard of it.'

'It was Wednesday last week. I believe there was quite a scare about it.'

'Wednesday?' said the man. 'That'll be Conway. Hang about.'

He went into an inner office and then another man came out. He only looked about twenty, hardly older than George's sixth-formers. George asked about the briefcase.

'It was brown leather, with the initials G. P. on it.'

'Yes, I remember,' said PC Conway. 'We nearly had the bomb squad in over that. Did you get it back all right?'

'Yes, thanks. They stole a watch out of it, that's all.'

'Good job they did,' said Conway. 'If we'd heard it ticking, that would have been the end of your briefcase.' He smiled.

George's first worry was over. Audrey had assured him that the transport police wouldn't have bothered going through the papers in the briefcase. They would just have handed it over to the regular police and let them locate the owner. It wasn't their department, she said. He didn't know how she knew this, but she was obviously right. The policeman was being pleasant and helpful. He didn't know about the photos.

'It was a funny business, that,' said Conway. 'It was standing right out in the open, as if we were supposed to find it.'

'I suppose they just wanted rid of it,' George said, 'once they saw there was nothing valuable.'

'So chuck it in a litter bin.' He shook his head. 'Funny business,' he said.

'Who handed it in?'

'Somebody spotted it. He was a taxi driver, I can tell you that much.'

This was a tricky bit. George didn't want to ask too many questions or seem too curious. If he had his briefcase back, it wouldn't make any difference who had reported it.

'I suppose you wouldn't have his name, by any chance? I'd like to say thank you. Maybe a reward.'

'I thought you said there was nothing valuable.'

Good point, George thought.

'Well, no, there wasn't, but, you know, at least he took the trouble to report it. That's quite something these days.'

Conway looked as if he might have been about to ask another question, then thought better of it.

'We should have a name,' he said, 'and a contact number or something.' He turned towards the door of the inner office. 'I'll see what I can find.'

The policeman had come up with a name and a phone number, but Stephen Leslie Martin was not an easy man to track down. Conway had said it was a daytime number so George assumed it was Mr Martin's workplace. He had managed to locate it by going into a post office and checking the number against all the entries for taxis in the Yellow Pages.

The minicab company was a shabby-looking affair, run on what seemed to be a pretty thin shoestring from a tiny office up a flight of rickety stairs. It consisted of a man behind a desk reading a newspaper, two telephone operators and a constant racket of calls coming in and going out. George asked about Stephen Martin.

'They're all out,' said the man, without looking up from his paper. He was a big man, bald except for a fuzz of grey above his ears, and with massive hands and forearms. He looked like a retired bouncer. 'They're all out on the road.' He looked up. 'What did you want him for?'

'He found something of mine,' George said. 'He handed it in to the police.'

The man gave George a look that was distinctly unfriendly. 'We always hand things in,' he said.

George had clearly given offence. This was a slur on the integrity of minicab drivers everywhere.

'Yes, yes, I'm sure you do. I just wanted to say thank you.'

George thought for a moment that the man was going to stand up and offer to defend the honour of the minicab profession, but he just returned to his newspaper.

'I'll tell him.'

'I'd like to tell him myself,' George said, 'if you don't mind.'

'End of shift,' said the man, without looking up from his paper. 'Six o'clock.'

George went home to wait until it was time to go back to the minicab company. He poured himself a drink and sat and thought about what Audrey had said.

It was simply incredible. It was incredible that there should be someone he knew, perhaps someone he had known for years, someone he worked with, who was capable of abusing and murdering a child and then trying to blame it on him. Wouldn't he recognize someone like that? Wouldn't it show? Could anyone hate him that much? Or perhaps it wasn't hatred. Perhaps there was no malice in it, nothing personal. As she had said, he was vulnerable, he was the ideal choice.

All sorts of silly ideas started going through his head. He wondered if he would recognize Stephen Martin. He wondered if he would go back to the cab company and find himself face to face with one of his colleagues moonlighting as a taxi driver. Prewitt, the knight of the road? Derek, the demon driver? Young Norman . . .

At half-past five he sat up in his chair and realized he had been asleep.

At six, he was back in the office. The man with the newspaper was still there, and now there were half a dozen drivers sitting around reading the papers and drinking tea out of pint mugs. Steve, it appeared, was still out on the road.

It was six thirty when he got back. He was a young man, mid-twenties, with a surly expression, cropped hair and an ear-ring in one ear. George was quite sure he had never seen him before. Martin had to complete some paperwork for the man at the desk, and then George introduced himself and asked about the briefcase. Martin was immediately on the defensive, as if he were being accused of something.

'Yes, I remember it. What about it?'

'Do you think we could talk outside?' George said. Everybody in the room was listening. 'It won't take a minute.'

They went outside and stood at the top of the stairs leading down to the street.

'I just reported it,' said Martin, 'that's all.'

'I know. I'm very grateful. You didn't see anybody near it, I suppose, anybody who might have put it there?'

'No.'

'What made you notice it?'

'I just noticed it, that's all. It was stood there a half-hour. I dropped off two fares. Why all the questions?'

'There was a watch stolen from it,' George said. 'I'd like to get it back.'

The man laughed. It was more a giggle than a laugh.

'You've got no chance,' he said.

'No, I suppose not. What made you go to the police?'

'That's what they're always saying, isn't it? There are notices all over the place. If you see something suspicious, tell the police.'

'Yes.'

'That's suspicious, isn't it? Just stood there.'

'Yes, I suppose it is.'

'Well, then.'

He was right, of course. He had seen something suspicious and he had reported it, as he was intended to do. Somebody had placed the briefcase where it was bound to attract attention and waited for it to be found. Somebody had placed it there unseen, stood watching unseen until it was reported, and then walked out of the station unseen. It could have been anyone. This was a dead end.

The man was obviously anxious to be getting away. There was no point in asking any more questions. He didn't know anything.

'Well, thanks for your time, anyway,' George said.

'Cheers,' said Martin.

Meanwhile, Audrey had been having a little more success with Cathy Pelham, though at first Cathy hadn't wanted to let her in. Audrey adopted the approach of the wife who needs to know just what sort of a bastard she'd lived with. It obviously struck a responsive chord. At the mention of divorce, the front door was opened wider.

'I haven't lived with him for nearly three years,' she said, 'but we were married a long time. You do understand? I have to know the truth.'

'We never know the truth,' said Cathy.

This was an interesting thought.

'I'm sorry,' Audrey said. 'I don't want to pry . . .'

'Mine's walked out on me for another woman. It's not a secret.'

'I'm so sorry.'

'We don't know what's going on when it's under our noses.' The door opened wider again. It's difficult to have a proper discussion of the iniquities of men with someone who is being kept standing on the doorstep.

'I know, my dear,' said Audrey, 'I know,' and she was in. They went through into the living-room.

'Sorry about the mess,' Cathy said. 'Alex leaves his stuff all over the place.' There was no mess. This was a woman who apologizes for the mess in her house in order to draw one's attention to the fact that there isn't any.

'Look,' Cathy said, 'coffee or something?'

'That would be lovely.'

Audrey sat down and made herself comfortable. The conversation could still go badly, and it's more difficult to throw someone out when they're sitting down and looking at home. Cathy went into the kitchen, came back into the living-room to collect cups and saucers from the sideboard, went into the kitchen again and then came back with coffee and biscuits. This was a good sign. The best china had come out.

Audrey watched her as she set out the coffee things. She was in her mid-thirties and extremely pretty. She could have passed for ten years younger and probably often did.

She was the sort of woman men want to take home and buy nice things for and protect. Audrey wasn't very sympathetic to this. She was the sort of woman who intimidated men. She had never met a man in her life who had shown the slightest interest in protecting her.

'There's no doubt about it in my mind,' Cathy was saying as she poured the coffee. 'I'm sorry, but there it is. He tried to get Alex into his car.'

'I don't suppose there's any in my mind, really,' Audrey said. 'I just wanted to hear it from you.'

'He said he'd give him a lift home. If that was all there was to it, why deny it? Why make Alex out to be a liar?'

'I'm not here to defend him,' Audrey said.

'I'm not saying he knew what he was doing. I mean, I don't suppose he planned it or anything.'

'I can't believe I've been so blind.'

'It was probably, you know, latent, repressed.'

'I'm sure you're right. I should have seen something, all the same. All those years.'

'I've been married for fifteen,' said Cathy. 'It took me ages to find out he had another woman.'

The ground rules for the conversation had been laid down. They were both nice women. They had both been wronged. They would not accuse each other of anything. Cathy would make excuses for George. Audrey would not. Cathy would not suggest that George was a monster and Audrey would not suggest that he was any less guilty than he appeared to be.

'It just worries me,' said Cathy, 'to think he's out there. What he might do. When you came to the door, I thought . . .'

'George won't come anywhere near you or Alex. I promise you that.'

'I don't think I could face it. It's not that I wish him any harm. I mean, I don't feel vindictive.'

'That's good of you.'

'He must have had some sort of breakdown.'

'Does your husband know about it?' Audrey said.

'No. We're not exactly on speaking terms at the moment.' She nibbled a biscuit. 'Alex is going to tell him this evening. I don't know why he couldn't have told him before.'

'It can't have been easy for you,' Audrey said.

'It's never been easy with Alex. He's very quiet. Introverted, I suppose you'd say. You never know quite what's going on in his head.'

'No.'

She suddenly seemed to be worried about what she might have said.

'He wouldn't lie to me, if that's what you're thinking,' she said fiercely. 'I know he wouldn't. Not about something like that.'

'No, of course not.'

'It's just that he lives in a world of his own so much of the time.'

'It must have been terrible for him.'

'He doesn't want to talk about it any more. I suppose that's why he wouldn't tell his father. Maybe it's for the best, if he can forget about it.'

'You're the one who needs to talk about it,' said Audrey, soothingly. 'It's so difficult with this sort of thing. Especially if you're alone. Was there anyone you could talk to?'

'I went straight to the headmaster as soon as it happened and told him the whole thing. He was very good about it.'

'I know Don,' said Audrey. 'I haven't seen him for years. He's very sympathetic.'

'I just told him the whole story and let him deal with it. He said I shouldn't talk to anyone about it. He was very good with Alex.'

Audrey didn't want to seem too inquisitive about who Cathy had talked to. She had already found out most of what she wanted to know.

149

'And all this on top of that other business,' she said. 'The little girl. It was this street, wasn't it?'

'It was right next door. She was supposed to go next door. She never turned up. Oh God, that was awful. It was pure chance I got mixed up in it. I'd never have known if I hadn't gone round.'

'You went next door?'

'Yes, to Val's. That's the woman next door. I just went round for a chat and a cup of coffee. Val was in a filthy mood because Daisy should have come for a fitting. I'd only been there about fifteen minutes when the mother arrived. Well, to cut a long story short, I ended up driving her round looking for Daisy. She was frantic.'

'I can imagine.'

'I was pretty desperate myself. The police took ages to arrive.'

'They always do,' said Audrey.

By the time they had finished their pot of coffee, Audrey needed no further explanation of Alex's stories. He was a little boy who lived in a world of his own and whose parents were in the middle of an acrimonious separation. He sounded exactly the sort of child who would make up stories about his teachers. The important question was, who knew? Don Prewitt had been told. The next step was to find out who he might have passed it on to. Cathy's husband didn't know, or so she claimed. She didn't seem to have told anyone else, though it was impossible to be sure. On the face of it, Don seemed the most likely channel for the story.

'You know, I'm glad you came,' Cathy said. 'We have a lot in common.'

'I'm glad I came too,' Audrey said.

17

In every murder investigation there are major leads, there
are minor leads and, always, there is one silly little piece
of evidence that doesn't connect with anything else and
doesn't make sense. The major lead, George Potter, had
led nowhere. The minor leads were being dealt with satis-
factorily. The thing that was keeping Rosewall awake at
night was the van.

It had been seen entering the lanes at eleven o'clock, an
hour after Daisy Beale's disappearance. A dark blue panel
van, or possibly green. The description was worthless.
Almost certainly it was entirely innocent and almost certainly the driver hadn't seen anything. What didn't make
sense was that he hadn't come forward.

He couldn't possibly not know that the police were looking for him. It had been on television, in the papers, everywhere. He couldn't not know that he had been in the lanes
that day and he couldn't not know what had happened
there. So where was he? What had he been doing? Com-
mitting a burglary? Visiting somebody's wife?

'Find that bloody van,' said Rosewall. 'I don't care where
you get the men from. Just find it.'

'Excuse me,' said the woman at the front door, in the
aggressive tone of somebody who says 'Excuse me' when
you have just stepped on their foot, 'are you Potter?'

'Yes.'

If it hadn't been for the fact that she knew his name,
George would have assumed that she was about to ask

him if he were familiar with the Lord. She was a woman in her early fifties, rather shabbily dressed in an overcoat that had seen better days and an absurd hat. She stood four-square in the doorway and eyed him malevolently. Collecting for a jumble sale, he decided. No, it couldn't be that. She knew his name.

It was nine o'clock in the morning and George was up and dressed and had had his breakfast. This had been touch and go. Why he had bothered to get up at all was another question.

'I'm the grandmother,' the woman said.

'Whose grandmother?'

'Our Daisy.'

George wasn't at his most alert in the mornings but he had the sense to try to shut the door. She had her foot in it. She had stuck her foot out and jammed it in the doorway just as he was closing the door. He had thought it was just an expression. He had never met anybody before who literally went around sticking their foot in the door. Before he knew what was happening, she had pushed the door open, barged in and pursued him into the house.

'I just want to know one thing from you,' she said. 'What did you do to her? What did you do to our Daisy?'

'Nothing.'

'What did you do, you beast?'

'Get out,' he said, 'or I'll phone the police.'

'Phone them. They know all about you.'

He couldn't have phoned. She was between him and the phone.

'They know I had nothing to do with it.'

'I want to look into your eyes,' she said. She did so. She just stood there, not moving, staring at him.

George glanced behind him. The bedroom door was open. He could get in there and shut the door. He began edging backwards. She followed him, slightly stooped with her feet wide apart, shuffling sideways to cut off his retreat like a wrestler circling the ring. Her eyes were fixed on him. George suddenly dived the other way.

'I have to go out,' he said. 'Sorry.' He grabbed his jacket off the back of a chair and made for the door.

George fled out into the street, putting his jacket on as he went. He didn't know where the woman was. He looked round. She was right behind him. He was walking as quickly as he could and she was a few paces behind him.

'Tell me what you did.'

She was screaming at him. People in the street stopped to look at them.

'Tell me what you did to Daisy.'

There was a newsagent's on the corner. She wouldn't follow him into a shop, surely. He pushed the door open and went in. A bell tinkled on the door. There were no other customers. He went up to the man at the counter and asked for a box of matches.

The bell tinkled again on the door.

'He killed her. He's the one killed Daisy.'

The man behind the counter looked at George, looked past him at the figure in the doorway and looked at George again.

'Twelve p.,' he said.

George grabbed his box of matches, fumbled in his pocket for change and threw a pound coin on to the counter. He turned and rushed out of the door, pushing the woman aside.

When he was out in the street, he broke into a run. A bus came past and slowed down in the traffic. He jumped on to it, twisting his ankle. Everybody on the bus turned to look at him.

When he was sitting down in his seat getting his breath back, he risked a look out of the window. The woman was standing on the pavement. He could hear her screaming.

'Beast! Beast!'

It was early evening when George came sneaking back to the house. He could hear the phone ringing as he came up to the door. He had been in a pub for most of the day, then he'd gone for a walk, then he'd been in another pub. He'd been freezing cold. He didn't have an overcoat.

The front door wasn't properly closed. He fully expected to have been burgled, but a glance round told him that everything seemed to be all right. The phone had stopped ringing. He went round the house checking in all the rooms, wardrobes, cupboards. At least she wasn't lurking in the house. He locked the front door and put the chain on.

He went into the kitchen and found a bottle of Scotch. It was medicinal. His ankle was hurting.

The phone rang again and he came through and answered it.

'Hello?'

'Is that George Potter?'

'Yes.'

'This is John Pelham,' said a very angry voice. 'I just want you to understand one thing, Potter. If you ever come anywhere near my son again, I'll come round there and I'll –'

George put the phone down, then picked the receiver up and left it off the hook. He took his bottle of Scotch and a glass upstairs, poured himself a drink and lay on the bed. His ankle hurt like hell. He managed to get his shoe off and it felt a little better.

He lay looking up at the ceiling. He was beginning to feel warmer now that he was inside the house and he had his whisky. He reviewed his position. Although exonerated of murder, he was on police record as a purchaser of child pornography and an enticer of little boys into cars. He had no job and little hope of ever having a job again. On top of that, he had the prospect of receiving threatening phone calls while he was in the house and being pursued down the street by Madame Defarge every time he went out of it. That seemed to cover it.

He had another drink of whisky. Beyond his immediate situation, what was there? One marriage, failed. No children. The book he had always intended to write, unwritten. Several generations of children, now adults, who still felt a shiver down their spines when they thought of him, if they did. Current meaningful relationships, nil. Future prospects, nil. Chances of finding himself assisting the police with their enquiries on numerous occasions, ample. Was he perhaps overlooking some positive aspect of his life? No.

He thought of Audrey. It had been nice seeing her again. Now that he wasn't married to her, he liked her.

He could no longer remember how or why it had all gone wrong. There had been a time, two, three years ago, when all he had wanted was to get away from her. He could remember feeling that way but he couldn't remember what had caused it. When he tried to remember her offences, or his, they seemed trivial.

There had been a time when it had been very different, when he had loved her, when he had hated being away from her, when he had listened for her footsteps outside the door each time she was away from the house. There had been a time when she had loved him, when she had found him exciting and funny and wise.

It had changed slowly. There had been love and then, little by little, there had not been love. There should have been something left when the love was gone. There should have been companionship, at least. There was nothing. It was not that they fought or argued. They could not be bothered. They had argued far more when they were young and in love. They argued more now. They argued when they liked each other. When the love had gone, there had been nothing left but an emptiness, a surface of amiability over a void.

Perhaps if there had been children . . .

He had even been enthusiastic about teaching once. He had drifted into it and then he had found that he was good at it. He could perform well in front of a class. He could entertain. He could hold their attention. He could let them wander off into their own worlds of discovery and bring them back to him whenever he wanted. But, years ago, something had gone wrong with that too. He had done it too often, day after day, term after term, year after year. The performance had hardened into a routine and the routine into a parody. The face had hardened into a mask.

He heaved himself off the bed, hobbled into the bathroom and came back with a bottle of aspirin. He placed it on the bedside table and poured himself another drink. He put the glass down and tried to unscrew the cap on the aspirin bottle. It just kept turning and clicking. It was childproof. He pushed the cap down, squeezed and turned it.

Norman was round at Val's again. It had been going on for three evenings now. After they had killed the kittens and he had kissed her, they had gone into the house and sat and talked for an hour or two about the school and George. His feeling of power had gone. Val was in control. He sat on the sofa beside her and he was allowed to kiss her if he wanted, but not without asking. Then he went home. On the second evening she had removed her top and allowed him to kiss her breasts. That was all. This evening it had been the same.

'That's enough for you now, Norman,' she said. 'You'll have to be a good boy for a while.'

He wanted to give himself to her as a lover and a friend. This way it was horrible, but not to have gone on seeing her would have been worse. He had considered raping her. Tonight he had thought she was waiting to see if he would, as if it were the next stage in the game.

She made it quite clear to him in their conversations that she had had lovers. Not relationships, merely lovers. A lot of them.

'What's wrong with that?' she said. 'Personally, I've never met a man who was much use the morning after. Most of them can't even make breakfast.'

So why not him? She was the first woman he'd got close to who hadn't laughed at him, the first woman he had really known who had taken him seriously. Now what was he to think? Why was she doing this to him? This was worse than being laughed at. This was hell.

What is the definition of a husband? thought Audrey Potter. A husband is a man you get out of bed and open the door to when he's blind drunk at two o'clock in the morning.

'You'd better come in,' she said, still pulling her dressing-gown on.

George fell in.

'I've hurt my ankle,' he said.

'So I see.'

She had to put her arm round him and half carry him to get him through into the living-room and on to the sofa. He sprawled backwards and put his foot up on the coffee table.

'Have you really hurt it,' she said, 'or are you just pissed?'

'Both. Is there anything to drink?'

'In your case, coffee.'

She helped him get his overcoat off, then knelt beside the table, lifted his foot up and took his shoe and sock off. The ankle was bruised and swollen.

'Looks like gangrene,' he said.

'Shut up,' she said. 'Don't wag it about.'

She put the fire on, then disappeared upstairs for ten minutes and there was some banging about from the floor above. When she came down, she went into the kitchen and put a pot of coffee on, filled a bowl with hot water and disinfectant and brought it through into the living-room. She rolled up his trouser leg and stuck his foot in the bowl. George groaned.

'Is that any better?'

'No.'

'You'd better see a doctor tomorrow,' she said. 'I think it's only a sprain.'

Half an hour later, the room had warmed up and George had had three cups of black coffee, told her about his conversation with the taxi driver and his encounter with Granny Beale, and soaked his foot. He was also beginning to sober up, which was not an improvement. His head throbbed. Audrey was sitting in one of the armchairs with her feet curled up underneath her. She had been telling him about Cathy Pelham.

'How are you feeling now?' she said.

'Awful.'

'You're looking a bit better. At least half human. I was worried about you.'

'What am I going to do?' he said, taking his foot out of the bowl and placing it gingerly on the floor.

'Stay here for the time being. I've made a bed up. You can't go back there with some mad woman chasing you round the streets.'

'I don't mean tonight. What am I going to do?'

'What can we do?' She made herself more comfortable in her chair. 'We just go on as we're going. All right, you drew a blank with the briefcase. At least I got somewhere with the Pelham woman.'

'You got nowhere,' he said, 'absolutely nowhere.' He put his foot up on the table again. 'The boy makes things up. We knew that. She told Prewitt about it. We knew that too. You got nowhere.'

She sat for a while, just looking at him.

'It's a start,' she said. 'The next thing is to find out who Don told.'

'If he told anybody. If he remembers.'

'It's worth a try.'

'No, it's not. Do you know what I thought of doing tonight? Do you know what I nearly did?'

'Oh, go to bed,' she said. 'We're both exhausted and we're not thinking properly.'

'You mean I'm not thinking properly. I'll tell you what I'm thinking. I think it's bloody hopeless. I don't know why we're chasing round talking to people. They don't know anything.'

'Go to bed, George,' she said. 'I'm tired and I can't cope with self-pity at this time of night. If I sit up listening to this any longer I'll probably break your other leg.' She stood up. 'The spare room's the first on the left. If you're going to fall over, do it quietly.'

She went upstairs. George sat for a few minutes, then hauled himself to his feet and hobbled up to the spare room. He managed to get undressed and into bed and he was asleep in seconds.

When he woke up, he knew he was going to be sick. He didn't know what time it was but it was still pitch dark. He turned the light on. His vision of the room billowed towards him in waves which thudded deep inside his brain and were sucked back to be replaced by other waves. The vomit rose in his throat and his cheeks burned. He cupped his hand to his mouth and rushed into the bathroom. He was violently sick two or three times.

When he thought he wasn't going to be sick any more, he put the cover down on the toilet seat and sat on it. The bathroom floor was freezing cold against his bare feet. He hadn't had time to put anything on.

There was a knock at the door.

'Can I come in?'

'No.'

She came in anyway. She stood looking at him for a few moments.

'Clean yourself up and come downstairs,' she said. 'I'll make you some weak tea.'

He got up and washed his face. He stood back from the mirror and looked at himself. His belly looked like a beanbag and his skin had the texture of a plucked chicken's.

'Potter,' he said, 'you're disgusting.'

He went into the bedroom and put his shirt and trousers on and then came downstairs. She was sitting in her armchair in the living-room and his cup of tea was on the table.

'Sorry about that,' he said, sipping his tea. 'What time is it?'

'About four.'

'Go back to bed if you like.'

'It's all right,' she said. 'I'm obviously not going to get any sleep tonight. How's the foot?'

He hadn't thought about his foot. He realized he'd stopped limping. He wiggled his toes.

'Can't feel a thing.'

'Anaesthetized,' she said.

He had another sip of his tea. He was actually beginning to feel a bit better.

'All that stuff you were saying the other day,' he said, 'about it being someone close to me, do you still believe that?'

'Of course.'

'We have to go on, then.'

She laughed.

'That's rich,' she said. 'I thought it was all hopeless.'

'I'm sorry. You were right. I wasn't thinking before. I mean it now. I want to go on. I have to. Please.'

He had no choice but to go on. Having failed to take his aspirin and whisky, he had no alternative. And he couldn't do it alone. If she turned him down now, he was finished. He would go down on his knees and beg if he had to. What did he have to lose? Pride? Dignity? It's difficult to feel dignified when you're sitting in a crumpled shirt and trousers and bare feet and you've just thrown up in somebody's bathroom.

'You'll have gone off the idea again in the morning,' she said.

'No, I won't. I can't do it on my own. I need help. Please.'

18

'Don!' said Audrey. 'It's been ages.'

She had bumped into Don Prewitt in the street while she was out doing her Saturday morning shop. This had not been easy. When George finally dragged himself out of bed, she had asked him if he knew where the headmaster did his shopping. After complaining about the state of his head and the state of his foot and whining about breakfast and insisting that he didn't have the faintest idea, he had remembered seeing Don in the supermarket near the school one Saturday.

Audrey had given him his breakfast and then she went and installed herself in a shop doorway near the super-market and waited. She'd spent what seemed like hours hovering in doorways and peering up and down the street like a tart looking for clients. At my age, she thought. The things I do for that man.

From Don's first reaction, he might have had the same impression of her intentions. Then recognition began to dawn.

'It's . . .'

'Audrey,' she said. 'Audrey Potter.'

'Audrey, of course. Why, it's been years.'

He had aged a lot since the last time she'd seen him and his stoop was more exaggerated. The affair with George and the Pelham boy had taken its toll, or something had, though he still looked like the same decent old buffer who couldn't remember where he'd been ten minutes ago.

'Don,' she said, 'could you do me an awful favour? Are you in a hurry? Do you have the car?' She picked up her shopping bags and dumped them noisily on the pavement to indicate the weight. Filling so many had been expensive but there were a lot of cans of cheap soup in the bottom by way of ballast. 'I can't get a taxi anywhere.'

He dithered a bit.

'Yes, yes, of course.'

'It's awfully good of you.'

Before Prewitt had a chance to change his mind, he had his hands full of shopping bags, she had slipped her arm through his, and they were on their way to the car-park.

'How's Sally these days?' she said when they were in the car. 'I've been meaning to come and see her.'

'She's fine. Well, not up and about or anything, but she's fine.'

'Oh, I am glad. And what has been going on at Weston Secondary? The police came to see me. What's my dread-ful ex. been getting up to? You must tell me all about it.'

By the time they got to Audrey's house and he had helped her in with the shopping, he was still only half-way through his story. She had told George to get out of the house as soon as he'd finished his breakfast and to go to the doctor's about his ankle and to keep out of the pubs. While Don was carrying the shopping in, she had a check around to make sure there wasn't an incriminating sock under the sofa.

'Stay and have a coffee,' she said. 'This is fascinating.'

He seemed to be about to say no.

'Please,' she said.

'Well, just for a minute.'

'George and little boys. How wonderful. I don't believe it.'

'It wasn't wonderful at all,' said Don. 'Not for the boy, not for the mother. It wasn't wonderful for me, I can tell you. I had the police round to see me too. There were all sorts of stories going round the school.'

'Oh, Don, I'm so sorry.' She settled him on the sofa. 'I'm being insensitive.' She went into the kitchen and came back with coffee and biscuits. 'It must have been dreadful for you,' she said. 'What did you do?'

'Well, I did what I could. I interviewed the boy. I talked to George. I tried to find out the truth. Then the police took over. There was nothing more I could do.'

The headmaster was terribly agitated. Either it upset him to talk about it, or he was worried about being away from Sally, or something. He seemed anxious to go, but she was determined he wasn't going anywhere. She hadn't finished with him yet.

'And there was nobody you could talk to,' she said, sympathetically. 'I mean, you couldn't really talk it over with anybody, could you? Except Sally, of course.'

'Well, exactly. If that sort of thing had got out, it could have been the ruin of the school. I suppose it will be now. I talked to Sally, as you say. And I prayed, Audrey. I don't mind telling you, I prayed. Sally and I both did. We prayed for George.'

'He doesn't deserve it,' she said.

'I can't believe he's lost,' said Don. 'I can't believe he's a lost soul.'

'It must have been a terrible temptation just to get it off your chest with somebody.'

'Who could I talk to? A story like that could finish the school. If it got in the papers . . . Well, it has now, of course. They haven't got the name of the school but . . .'

'Derek?' she said.

'I didn't even mention it to Derek. I couldn't bring myself to talk about it, quite honestly. Well, not until after the arrest. Then it was all over the school. You can imagine.'

This was getting her nowhere. It was the same problem she'd had with Cathy Pelham. Nobody had said anything to anybody. She ran through the list of people in her mind who knew about Alex's stories. Cathy. She had told no one except Don, not even her husband. So, Don, Sally. Not Derek. So, presumably, not Pris either. Don had told God. That was it.

Someone was lying, or had told someone else and forgotten. Audrey had no doubt that someone had known about Alex's stories, someone who had seen his opportunity and had calmly set about framing her husband for murder, a murder he had himself committed.

'I'm going to have to run,' said Don, jumping up from his chair and leaving half his coffee. 'Sally gets so worried . . .'

'Of course. Thanks for the lift. Lovely to see you again.'

'You must come round some time. I'm quite a cook these days.'

'I'd love to.'

She saw him out to the front door. He turned in the doorway and looked at her.

'Who could I tell?' he said. 'Who?'

*

'Have you had a terrible day, darling?' Derek said. 'You're looking tired.'

Although it was Saturday, Pris had had a lot of work on and she had had to go into the office for most of the day.

'You mean haggard,' she said.

'No, darling, I didn't. Honestly. Oh God.'

Val had invited Norman and the Hodges to dinner. Derek had arrived early and had drunk a bottle of wine by the time Pris arrived. Norman had also drunk a bottle of wine. It was obvious from his behaviour that Derek believed Norman was now living at Sefton Road, or at least that he and Val were sleeping together. Why? Had she told him? She certainly wasn't doing anything to suggest it wasn't true. She kept smiling at Norman and she rested her hand on his shoulder each time she went past his chair. Was this the latest game?

As soon as Pris arrived, they sat down to dinner. Val made a special fuss of serving Norman. Derek pretended not to notice. Pris stared. Norman wished he could die.

Once they had started eating, the conversation turned to George.

'He's been seeing the wife again, apparently,' said Pris. 'Isn't that what you heard?'

'I certainly did.'

'I don't know how she can let him in the house, a man like that. He's probably violent. Inadequate men usually are. I don't understand women like that.'

'They're just trapped, darling,' said Derek, 'trapped.' He reached across the table rather unsteadily with the bottle, topped up the glasses and refilled his own.

'She's not. There are none of the usual problems you get with battered wives. God knows, I've seen enough of them. She's got her own house. No kids to worry about. There's nothing to stop her shutting the door in his face.' She took a mouthful of food and a sip of her wine. 'I can't stand violent men. If Derek ever touched me like that, I'd kill him.'

'I'd want you to,' said Derek. His glass was nearly empty again. 'I really would. You do believe me, darling?'

'I'm told it can be quite fun,' said Val, 'provided everyone knows the rules. You have to have a signal for when you really want it to stop.'

She smiled broadly across the table at Norman. Pris stopped eating and stared. So it was the latest stage in the game. Everyone was supposed to believe they spent every night thrashing the bed to pieces, and only he would know the truth.

'Castration's the answer,' said Derek, slicing through his steak. 'I've always said so. Chop it off.'

'There are problems with that too, of course,' said Pris, thoughtfully. 'It takes away the means but not the desire. It can just make them more violent.'

'I'd have it done,' said Derek. 'I'd do it myself if I thought I was a danger to anyone. I really would.'

'Most men aren't violent,' said Norman. He was getting tired of all this. 'I've never come across it. Most of the women I know don't look battered.'

'The real problem isn't violent men,' said Pris, glaring at him. 'The real problem is men. Look at the world. What do you see? Rape. Murder. Child abuse. And who's in charge? Who's got all the power? Men. Personally, I'd never let a man near a child, any man. Not fathers, not brothers, not any of them.'

'Not all men are rapists,' said Norman, bitterly. He looked across the table at Val. She just smiled at him.

'We are,' said Derek, filling his glass up again, 'we are. I'm a rapist. You're a rapist. We're all rapists. We can't get enough of it. God, why is the male sex so bloody awful?'

*

On Sunday morning, Rosewall was up bright and early. They had found somebody else who'd seen the van, and this time they had something better than a description. They had the registration number. They had put every available man on to it, much to the disgust of Rosewall's superiors, and it had paid off. They had gone back to every house in the neighbourhood of the lanes. They had questioned everybody again, this time specifically about the van, and they had found Mr Jellicoe. They'd missed him before because he had been in hospital.

'You'd better go easy with him, sir,' said the PC who opened the front door. 'He's about a hundred and he's as batty as a coot.'

'Thank you, constable,' said Rosewall.

Mr Jellicoe lived in the end house where the lanes met the main road, at the opposite end from where Daisy had disappeared, at the end which was wide enough for traffic to enter.

Rosewall showed himself through into the living-room. Mr Jellicoe was a gaunt old man, probably in his eighties. He was sitting in an armchair in his dressing-gown. He seemed very frail but the look in his eyes was sharp enough.

'Who are you?' he said.

Rosewall identified himself and produced his warrant card. Mr Jellicoe took the card and scrutinized it through a magnifying glass which was kept handy on the table beside the armchair. His hand shook slightly. The glass seemed almost too heavy for him. The skin on the backs of his hands looked paper thin, hardly strong enough to contain the veins.

Mr Jellicoe took his time examining the card, glancing up at Rosewall from time to time. The old man was demonstrating that if anyone imagined he was in less than full possession of his faculties, they had another think coming.

Rosewall waited patiently. Mr Jellicoe was eventually satisfied and handed back the card.

'What do you want?'

'I understand you took down the registration number of a van, sir.'

'Registration number?' said the old man, in a voice that had suddenly become almost a squeak. 'You want registration numbers?'

He got up stiffly from his armchair, with Rosewall's assistance, went over to a desk, opened a drawer and took out a pile of exercise books, at least a dozen of them. He came back and dropped them on the table with a look of triumph and sat down again.

'Have a go at that lot,' he said.

Rosewall picked up the first book and opened it. It was a school exercise book, narrow-ruled. On each line, in minute but remarkably legible handwriting – no wonder he needed the magnifying glass – there was a date entirely in Roman numerals and the time of day, followed by a registration number, followed by a brief description of a vehicle. Rosewall flicked through the other books. They were all the same. He looked quizzically at Mr Jellicoe.

'The robberies,' said the old man, as if it should be blatantly obvious even to a policeman. 'Thousands of them round here. Day and night.'

'And these numbers are . . .?'

'Anything suspicious, I write it down. I see them coming past the house, front and back. Anything suspicious, down it goes.'

Rosewall found the appropriate book and started searching for the date of Daisy's disappearance.

'They were in next door last week,' said Mr Jellicoe, 'when I was in hospital. Made off with the wireless and God knows what. I'd have had their number if I'd been here.'

Rosewall was still flicking through the pages of the exercise book, trying to remember how Roman numbers worked.

'And what are your lot doing about it?' the old man said.

'We do what we can, sir.'

'Bugger all,' said Mr Jellicoe, 'that's what your lot are doing about it. I don't know what you get paid for.'

Rosewall had found the entry he was looking for.

10.50 a.m. E 237 LOT. Blue van.
11.02 a.m. Back he comes.

'The van entered the lanes at ten fifty,' said Rosewall. 'Is that right?'

'If that's what it says.'

'And it would have gone out of your line of sight?'

'Course it would.'

'And it returned twelve minutes later?'

'Whatever it says in the book.'

'These times are reliable?'

The old man nodded towards a clock on the mantelpiece.

'Never wrong these forty years,' he said. 'I check it by the wireless every Sunday and wind it up. They don't make them like that. It's all Japanese now. Rubbish with batteries in.'

'You don't remember catching a glimpse of the driver, by any chance?'

Mr Jellicoe shook his head.

'Wouldn't remember if I did.'

'Do you mind if I keep this, sir?'

'Keep the lot,' said Mr Jellicoe. 'They're all there. Anything suspicious, I write it down.'

'Well, thank you for your co-operation. You've been very helpful. I wish we had more witnesses like you.' Rosewall rolled up the exercise book and put it in his pocket. 'I'll see myself out.'

The old man let him get almost to the front door.
'Bugger all,' he said, 'that's what.'

19

Rosewall shuffled the papers in front of him, opened Mr Jellicoe's exercise book at the appropriate page and looked across the table in the interview room. Sitting beside him was one of the sergeants on the Daisy Beale case, who was taking notes. Sitting opposite him was Stephen Leslie Martin, minicab driver and registered owner of the van E 237 LOT.

He looked harmless enough. He wore the uniform of the young semi-skilled male – cropped hair, one ear-ring, denim shirt and jeans. He was surly, but that could have been nerves. He wasn't backward by any means, Rosewall had decided, but he wasn't especially bright either. They hadn't found a criminal record but they were still looking.

He had been traced to a two-room rented flat above a bookmaker's shop on the estate, a few streets away from where Daisy had lived. The blue van was parked outside. It was Sunday afternoon, his day off work, and they had got him out of bed. When he was asked to come to the police station, he had seemed puzzled and defensive but he had been ready to help as soon as he was told that it concerned the murder of a little girl.

Rosewall was taking it very gently. It was an informal interview, just a chat to discover whether Martin was in possession of any information that might be of use. The only grounds they had for being suspicious of him was that he hadn't come forward in response to police appeals to the public. It could be something and it could be nothing.

'You were driving the van that day?' Rosewall said.

'I've said I was.'

'What were you doing in the lanes?'

'Out for a drive. It was my day off that week, Saturday.'

'Why the lanes?'

'Short-cut.'

'It's a dead end,' said Rosewall.

'Some of them lanes,' said Martin, 'you can get out the other end. Some you can't. I don't know which is which.'

'But you're a taxi driver.'

'Doesn't mean I have to know everything.'

He was tense. He sat rigidly in his chair with his hands clasped tightly in front of him on the table, occasionally flexing his fingers. His gaze flickered around the room each time he spoke but he never looked directly at Rosewall. His way of answering questions was truculent, as if he had already been unjustly accused of something. For someone who was merely being interviewed as a possible witness, he was too much on the defensive.

'All right,' Rosewall said, 'tell me what happened in the lanes.'

'I drove in, realized it was a dead end, backed out.'

'How long did that take, do you think?'

'I don't know. Five minutes, ten minutes. They're narrow, them lanes. It was tricky getting out.'

'Did you see anything out of the ordinary, hear anything?'

'No. I was busy trying to get out, wasn't I?'

It wasn't that he was being unhelpful, exactly. He hadn't refused to answer a question. He just wasn't saying a word more than he had to. Rosewall was sure he was hiding something, and equally sure that it would take a lot more than one interview to find out what it was.

'Why didn't you come forward?'

'No reason. Never saw anything, did I?'

'That doesn't matter. You were there.'

'Never heard about it.'

171

'Never heard about what?' said Rosewall. 'Never heard about the murder? Never heard about the appeals to the public?'

'Yeah,' said Martin, 'appeals.' He looked up at the ceiling. 'I've heard about the murder. Course I have. Everybody has.'

'You didn't know about the appeal for witnesses?'

'No.'

'It was on television,' said Rosewall. 'It was in the papers. We had posters up all over the town. Anyone in the lanes that day to contact the police.'

'I haven't got time to read the papers,' said Martin, gazing round the room.

This was getting them nowhere. Rosewall didn't believe a word of it but there wasn't much he could do about it at the moment. If Martin said he hadn't heard about the appeals, he hadn't heard about them. They couldn't prove he had. He had been in the lanes that morning for twelve minutes, according to Mr Jellicoe's clock. It was rather a long time just to drive in, go far enough to realize his mistake and back out, but he had said it was difficult getting out. He had seen nothing, heard nothing. He had no information. Besides, he was there an hour too late, unless Daisy had wandered off somewhere and then come back.

Rosewall stood up.

'I won't keep you any longer, then, Mr Martin.'

Martin looked at him for the first time and shot up out of his chair.

'Thanks for coming in on a Sunday. You will let us know if you remember anything, anything at all?'

'Yeah, course,' said Martin. 'Cheers.'

Rosewall watched as the sergeant showed him out of the room, then he slowly collected up his papers. After a minute or two, the sergeant put his head round the door.

'I want to know everything about him,' Rosewall said. 'I want to know where he went to school. I want to know if he was a good little boy. I want to know who his parents are. I want to know what he has for breakfast and how many teeth his granny's got left.'

Rosewall had driven out to the lanes, near to the place where Daisy had disappeared. He was sitting in his car, parked at the end of Sefton Road. He had needed to get out of the station for a while and just sit on his own somewhere quiet and think.

The most likely explanation for Martin's behaviour was that he had a criminal record, possibly something his employer didn't know about, and he didn't want anything to do with the police. If so, they would find out. Either that, or he had been up to something in the lanes that morning which he didn't want anyone to know about, possibly something perfectly legal.

The other possibility, of course, was that he was connected with the little girl's disappearance, but Rosewall couldn't see how. He had been there an hour too late. It was impossible to believe that Daisy had wandered the streets for an hour, unseen by anyone, and then come back to Sefton Road to be abducted. Three witnesses had placed the van in the lanes around eleven o'clock, and Rosewall would not have dared question the reliability of Mr Jellicoe's clock.

Assuming that Daisy had been abducted at ten, it was still incredible that no one had seen or heard anything. Rosewall looked up and down the road. It was deserted now except for an old man pottering about in his front garden a few doors down from where he was parked, but this was Sunday afternoon. Even now there was somebody about. Daisy had disappeared in the middle of a Saturday morning. A little girl being led through the streets, probably in tears, or being bundled into a vehicle . . .

Rosewall got out of his car and walked to the place where the lane came out into the road, the place where Daisy had disappeared, two doors away from the Pelham boy's house. Here was a coincidence. Daisy had vanished practically outside the Pelham house and it was the Pelham boy who had put them on to George Potter. No, there was no point in thinking along those lines. It was coincidence and nothing more.

He looked down the lane towards the corner of the garden wall where it branched right and left. Daisy had come from the right. He imagined her coming round the corner and running towards him with her head down. She looked up for a moment, saw him, stopped running and smiled. He smiled. He still believed what he had believed all along. It had to be someone she knew, someone she trusted, someone she would happily go away with.

When he got back to his car, there was a call from the station. They had an address for Stephen Martin's parents.

'He's not in any trouble?' said Mrs Martin. 'He's always been such a good boy.'

'No trouble at all, madam,' said Rosewall. 'It's just routine.'

Routine? Routine what? What sort of routine? He had expected them to query this but they didn't. The Martins were people who trusted the police and didn't question what they were told. Rosewall hadn't realized that there were people like that left any more.

Stephen Martin's parents lived in a small terrace house on the estate. Rosewall had been in scores of houses like this in his time. He could have found his way around blindfold. A front room, a dining-room, a kitchen, three bedrooms upstairs. All these houses looked the same.

People tried to personalize them but the more they were personalized the more they resembled one another because everybody personalized them in the same way.

Rosewall, it seemed, had narrowly avoided interrupting Sunday lunch. Mrs Martin was clearing the dining-room and laying out tea in the front room. Mr Martin was having a pipe. They were older than Rosewall had expected. They were both grey-haired and plump and they looked remarkably alike. Mr Martin couldn't be far off retirement age. They must have been nearly into their forties when young Stephen was born.

Mrs Martin was flustered because she had a visitor before she had finished clearing the table. She closed the dining-room door to hide the fact that there were things still not cleared away, then she came and sat down in the front room with her husband. Rosewall was offered the most comfortable armchair and accepted a cup of tea.

'He was never any trouble,' said Mr Martin. 'Good as gold. You've got to be thankful after what he'd been through.'

Such a good boy? Good as gold? What age did they think he was?

'Oh,' said Rosewall, sipping his tea, 'what was that?'

'Well, the adoption,' said Mrs Martin. 'Of course you knew about that.'

'Yes, madam.' Rosewall hadn't known about it. People like the Martins assume the police can find out anything they want to know about anybody and quite right too. He wished they could. An adoption buried in the paperwork is almost impossible to detect, as it is intended to be.

'The father,' said Mr Martin, 'the natural father . . .' He hesitated for a moment, fiddled with his pipe and looked at his wife. 'Well, he wasn't very nice if you know what I mean.' Looks were exchanged between husband and wife. It had not been easy for him to say even this much.

'Yes, sir.' Not very nice? So, violence, presumably. Probably the other as well. This was not a house in which child abuse would be called by its name.

'The father would have been violent, then, sir? Is that what you're telling me?'

'Worse than that,' said Mr Martin.

'He was an animal,' said Mrs Martin. The effort of saying this seemed to have exhausted her. She sat back in her chair and stared down into her cup of tea.

'I see.' There was no point in trying to get them to be explicit. They couldn't be.

'I believe he was actually prosecuted,' said Mrs Martin, looking up. 'Went to prison, I think. It was a terrible business. So they were taken into care, you see. That's how we came to adopt him.'

'They?' said Rosewall. 'You said "they".'

'There were two of them, I think. I think there was a brother.' She looked at her husband. 'Wasn't there a brother?'

'I think so,' said Mr Martin. 'We never talk about it. We never talked to Stephen about his other family.'

'We're his family now,' said Mrs Martin.

'Yes, madam.' Rosewall took out his notebook. This was getting interesting. 'You don't know what happened to this brother?'

Mrs Martin looked at him reproachfully. He was a policeman and so entitled to ask whatever he liked, but had they not made it clear that these things were not spoken about? Hadn't more than enough been said already?

'I think he was adopted too,' she said tersely. 'Yes, I'm sure he was.'

Rosewall was scribbling in his notebook.

'So he'd have a different surname now?'

'I suppose so.'

'Does Stephen have any contact with this brother?'

'Oh, no,' said Mrs Martin, vehemently. 'I'm sure he doesn't. He would have said.' She was getting very agitated about all this talk of the other family, the wrong family.

'He just wants to put all that behind him,' said Mr Martin.

Easier said than done, Rosewall thought.

'Do you remember the name of Stephen's family?' he said. 'His natural family, that is.'

'Yes, of course I remember. It was Winter. Leslie Winter, he was.' Mrs Martin smiled. 'We kept the Leslie but we put Stephen in front, just to give him something of ours.'

'It sounds more distinguished,' said Mr Martin, 'two names.'

'Yes, sir, very nice.' Rosewall did not suggest that little Stephen Leslie might perhaps have failed to live up to the distinction.

'It's remarkable when you think about it,' said Mrs Martin, refilling the cups, 'how well he's turned out. Such a good boy.'

'Yes, madam.'

'Are you sure he's not in any trouble?'

'Quite sure. It's just routine.'

What Rosewall would have liked to ask them was exactly when the brothers had been adopted and everything they could remember about the prosecution of the father. There were a lot of things he would have liked to ask, but he had asked enough. He didn't want them to be alarmed and, in the light of what he'd heard, he didn't want them alerting young Stephen. Besides, they couldn't have talked about these things. They had no language in which to talk about them. Things had happened which were not nice. All that was needed was to say that they were not nice and then to forget them.

When Rosewall had completed his interview and drunk his tea, they chatted for a while about how well Stephen was doing in his job, and then he thanked them for their help and went out and sat in his car for some time before driving back to the station. He read through his notes. He was having to think everything through again from the beginning. He had to consider that they might have got all the times wrong.

He felt almost sorry for young Stephen. He could imagine what it must have been like for him coming to his new parents. They were the sort of people who would insist that babies were brought by storks, as if his life had been as innocent as their own. He had gone to live in the stifling niceness of a house where sexuality could not be spoken about, and he had come from a house where the whole of his young life had been sex.

Rosewall knew what he was looking at. What he had in front of him was a classic profile of an abuser.

When Rosewall got back to his office, he put through a call to one of the sergeants on the Daisy Beale case.

'Some time,' he said, 'between let's say the early seventies and the mid-eighties there was a child abuse case involving somebody called Winter. There may have been a conviction. I want the file on my desk.'

There was a pause at the other end of the line.

'There won't be anything on the computer,' said the sergeant. 'Not that far back. I'd have to go through everything by hand.'

'You'd better get started, then,' said Rosewall.

20

George came in at the main gate. The school floated in front of him in the moonlight like something seen in a mirage. Or perhaps it was George who was floating. He looked down at his feet to make sure. No, it was the school. It didn't seem quite fixed to the ground. It was moving gently like a ship at night held by invisible mooring ropes.

Contrary to Audrey's instructions, he had been in a pub. In fact, he had spent most of the afternoon and evening in a number of pubs. He'd had a long walk since coming out of the last one and it had done him good, cleared his head. He didn't remember much about it but he was sure it had done him good. His ankle wasn't hurting today. Audrey had been right. It had turned out to be just a sprain. He had been disappointed. He had derived a certain satisfaction from hobbling round heroically on a broken leg.

He had spent the morning in bed and in the afternoon he had been back to his own house for a change of clothes. He had begged Audrey to let him stay with her for a few more days in case Granny Beale were still lying in wait for him, and she had agreed. He had slunk back to his house, shoved a few clothes and a toothbrush into his briefcase, and come out. Then he had gone in the pub. That was hours ago.

He didn't know why he'd come to the school. He hadn't thought about coming. It was the first time he'd been here since the day his car had been broken into and his briefcase stolen. He had no business being here, but a Sunday evening was pretty safe. He wouldn't have dared come back on a weekday when there might be people about. He knew what they were all saying about him. It wasn't that he'd missed the place. He was glad to be away from it, to tell the truth. He just felt like having a last look at it.

George looked at the school. The school looked at George. He looked up at the dark windows, cocked his head on one side and winked at it. The school winked back.

No, really. Suddenly a patch of grass beyond the far corner of the school had become lit up, as though someone had switched a light on in one of the end classrooms, and the glow was thrown back on to the front of the building. By the time he had stumbled round to the corner, the light had gone. Everything was dark again. It must have been a trick of the moonlight.

He decided it was his duty to investigate, all the same. He went up to the main door and tried the handle. It was locked. He walked slowly round the school, looking up at the windows for any sign of a light, and reached the back door, which was only used by the staff and the caretakers. He tried the handle. The door opened with a creak. It was unlocked.

This was all right. Lots of people had keys. Prewitt had a key. The caretakers had keys. Members of staff could get keys if they needed to come back in the evening, though it was unusual on a Sunday. People were supposed to lock the door behind them when they went in and unlock it again when they came out, but they often didn't bother. Whoever it was, George didn't really want to meet any-body. He closed the door as quietly as he could.

He turned his back on the school and began walking towards the gate. So, if somebody was in there, why weren't there any lights on? There wasn't a light to be seen. He turned round and came back and walked along the front of the school again, looking up at the windows. He went to the corner and looked up at the window where he'd thought he'd seen a light before, then walked around the back again. It was completely dark and silent except for his footsteps crunching on the gravel path and the noise and lights of the occasional car passing in the street. There were no lights, not in the corridors, not in the classrooms, not in the staffroom. Either somebody had been there earlier and gone home and forgotten to lock the door, which was a capital offence, or somebody was still in there with all the lights off. He opened the door and went in.

He was at the back of the entrance hall. It was dark but he knew every inch of the school and he didn't need to put a light on. Besides, he didn't want to advertise his presence. Whoever was in there, if anybody was, they probably had more right to be there than he had, lights or no lights.

He walked slowly down one of the corridors that led away from the hall, looking in the empty classrooms and peering suspiciously into shadows and checking that all the doors were locked, and then he came back to the hall along another corridor. There was enough light coming in through the windows to see quite clearly. There was no sign of anybody. He was about to go upstairs to check the upper classrooms and the staffroom when he thought he'd better have a quick look in the assembly hall.

The hall was Prewitt's pride and joy and the best thing about the school. It was unusually big, big enough to seat the whole school, and it had a balcony and a proper stage.

As he came in through the double doors at the back of the hall, a seat banged in the balcony above his head. It gave him a shock – he nearly jumped out of his skin – but when he thought about it, there wasn't really anything to be worried about. The balcony seats were not wooden chairs like the ones in the body of the hall. They were fixed to the floor and sprang up when they weren't being used, like cinema seats. Sometimes they stuck when they had

181

been down for a long time and then sprang back up on their own.

The edge of the balcony overhung the back of the hall and he had to walk forward to about the middle of the hall before he could look up into it. It was quite a bit darker in here than out in the corridors. The windows were high up in the walls and didn't give as much light. He couldn't see anything at first. He was going to switch the lights on, but then he began to make out the outline of the rows of seats and the two doors at the back of the balcony. There was no one there. One of the doors, which led out on to the staircase down to the entrance hall, was standing open. This didn't mean anything. The doors were often left open.

He was beginning to feel ridiculous. Here he was creeping about in the dark in a school from which he was in effect banned when he should have been going back to Audrey's and going to bed, and all because he'd imagined he'd seen a light and he'd found a door open. So there was a door open. It wasn't his problem if there was a door open. It wasn't his problem if the whole school was being ransacked. He might even help with the ransacking.

He stood with hands on hips, looking up into the balcony, and shouted.

'Hellooo. Anybody there?'

There was no answer. His voice echoed briefly.

'Come out, come out, whoever you are.'

His head was beginning to swim. He was actually feeling rather dizzy standing there looking up, and he thought he might be in danger of falling over backwards. He regretted having gone on to shorts in the last pub. He grunted, looked around him and then made his way to the stage at the far end of the hall, knocking over a chair as he went.

He reached the stage, scrambled up the steps at the side and stood on the edge, looking around him. He could see quite well from up here. The moonlight was coming in through the windows high up in the hall. They'd been rehearsing a play or something. The table they used for assemblies had been pushed to the side and the stage was strewn with props and bits of home-made scenery and all kinds of stuff. Somebody would be in trouble for not clearing up on Friday.

He began kicking things. Oh, why not? If he did any damage, he wouldn't be here in the morning to find out what it was. He wouldn't ever be here again. Over at the side of the stage he walked into something that was hidden by the curtain. It was solid and about half his own height. He wondered briefly what it might be and kicked it as hard as he could. It landed with a tremendous clatter somewhere in the darkness behind the curtain.

George froze. There had been another noise. There had been the noise on stage and then, unmistakably, there had been another noise at the other end of the hall. He took a few steps forward, stood on the edge of the stage and looked towards the doors at the back. He couldn't put a light on because there were no switches at this end of the hall.

It was dark at the back of the hall and it was a moment or two before he could see. At first he wasn't sure what it was he could see, then he was sure. There was someone standing at the far end of the hall, just inside the doors, standing quite still, watching him. Somewhere outside the hall he heard a door shut.

'Who's there?'

George had come down the steps at the side of the stage. The man at the other end of the hall hadn't moved. George wasn't sure how he knew it was a man, but he knew. He could see him a little more clearly now. He was wearing dark-coloured clothes. George couldn't see his face. It was a burglar. It had to be.

There were no switches for the lights at the stage end of the hall. The switches were half-way down, on each side, and there were more beside the doors where the burglar was standing. If he hadn't been a burglar, he'd have switched the lights on.

'Who's there?'

The man didn't answer. George hadn't expected him to. There wasn't a sound in the hall except the ticking of the clocks. There were two clocks, one on either side of the stage. They always told different times and he noticed now that they ticked at slightly different speeds.

For a while they just stood and looked at each other. George knew the man was looking at him even though he couldn't see his face. Why didn't he make a run for it? There was nothing stopping him. He was between George and the door. All he had to do was slip out, across the entrance hall and through the back door. It was still open. George had no chance of catching him, even if he'd wanted to. Any burglar in his right mind would have been gone by now.

Suddenly the man was moving, but he was moving towards George. He had come forward to the first row of chairs and was padding slowly and silently along behind it, coming across on to George's side of the hall.

George switched the lights on. He didn't know how he'd reached the switches. He had been standing just below the stage and a second later he'd been half-way down the hall fumbling with the light switches. He didn't remember moving.

The lights buzzed with a high, singing whine above his head and then blazed out all around him. He couldn't see anything at first because he'd been in the dark too long. He thought the man had gone. Then suddenly he was right in front of him, just a few feet away, and George found himself looking into the face of the taxi driver Stephen Martin.

For a moment they stood and looked at each other. Martin looked up at the lights above his head and then looked back at George.

George never knew what the man hit him with. He took something out of his pocket and lunged forward and the pain exploded in the side of George's head. The man raised his arm again. George reached forward to grab the arm and his ankle twisted underneath him and he fell to his knees. He looked up, expecting another blow, but the man was backing away towards the wall. The lights went out.

George was up on his feet in a second. There was no feeling in his ankle but he knew that if he tried to fight it would give way again. He turned and half ran, half stumbled back towards the stage, knocking over chairs. His ankle gave out as he reached the steps.

He went up the steps on his hands and knees, crawled across the stage, found the edge of the stage curtain and hid behind it. Holding on to the edge of the curtain, he managed to stand up, keeping the injured foot off the ground. His ankle was throbbing now. His head was throbbing.

He put his hand up to his head. His hair felt wet. He tried to look at his hand but it was too dark to see and he was afraid to come out from behind the curtain. Something wet was running through his hair and down his neck. His shirt was sticking to his back below the collar. There was too much of it to be sweat. He was bleeding heavily.

He knew he was trapped. There was a door that led from backstage out into one of the corridors but it was on the other side and he would have to cross the open stage to get to it. The only other way out was back through the hall where the man was waiting for him. There was nowhere else to go.

He was wrapped in the outer curtain, which hung in folds at the edge of stage, with another curtain behind him. He was trying not to move and give his position away, and to keep his foot off the ground. He was afraid he was going to faint if he stayed here much longer. The curtain was pulled against his face and it smelt dank and musty. His head was swimming and he couldn't breathe properly without feeling sick.

He forced himself to take two or three deep breaths and tried to think. If Martin hadn't seen him go behind the curtain, he was fairly safe provided he didn't pass out. He remembered that when he'd been up on the stage before, he'd walked into something behind the curtain without seeing it. There wasn't enough light on stage to see behind the curtain. Switching the lights out had been Martin's big mistake. He had the advantage and he had a weapon. By switching the lights out he had given them almost an equal chance.

The feeling came out of nowhere – pure anger, deeper and blacker than he had ever felt before. Above the throbbing in his head and the nausea in his throat and stomach, it welled up inside him like the first surge of drunkenness. He knew his enemy. He understood. Martin hadn't found his briefcase. He had stolen it and he had put it there. He had put the photos in it. He had given it to the police. This man was the cause of everything. This was the man who had turned him into a criminal. This was the man who had covered his whole life in filth.

He was suddenly aware that Martin was very close to him. He must have come up the steps on the other side of the stage. George could hear him shuffling backwards and forwards. He didn't know exactly where George was. This was his chance.

He scrabbled around behind the curtain for a weapon, anything he could use. He bent down and swept his hand around the floor in as wide an arc as he could, still holding on to the curtain. His hand touched the edge of something and he groped along it and picked it up. It was long and round and hard like a broom handle or a piece of piping. He waited until he could hear the man poking about on the other side of the curtain, then he stepped out from behind it and swung his weapon as hard as he could.

He hit him on the chest or the shoulder. The man staggered back and almost fell. George hit him again, aiming for the head this time. There was a noise like air escaping from a rent in a tyre and the man crumpled on to the stage and moaned.

George tried to get to the steps but he couldn't move. His foot was caught in something, his bad foot. He tried to shake it free but something was pulling it back. Then he could see the man lying on the stage under the folds of the curtain, gripping his ankle with both hands. George kicked at the hands with his free foot but the man only groaned and gripped tighter. Then he kicked at the head, once, twice. The grip loosened. George reached the steps and fell down them. Martin had let go.

He got to the door of the hall after colliding with a few chairs and then out through the back door of the school. It was very dark and bitterly cold outside. He made his way slowly round to the front of the school. It was all he could do to walk now, dragging his injured foot behind him.

There was no traffic on the road, no one to get help from. He was afraid to touch his head but the side of his face was wet and sticky.

21

It was nearly one o'clock in the morning when Rosewall's phone rang. He'd only just got to sleep. He switched the light on and picked up the receiver.

'I'll take it on the other phone,' he said. 'Hold on.'

He got out of bed and put his slippers and dressing-gown on, then switched the light off.

'I'll take it downstairs,' he said to his wife. 'You go back to sleep.'

'I already have,' she said.

He went downstairs and picked up the receiver. He listened for a few moments.

'They're still in pursuit?' he said.

He listened again.

'Get somebody round to the flat now,' he said. 'I want it taken apart. I'll be there in half an hour.'

He put the phone down and went into the kitchen to put the kettle on. He wasn't doing anything else until he'd had a cup of tea. He had a feeling it was going to be a long day.

Twenty minutes earlier, George had been in a phone box calling the police. He told them Daisy Beale's killer was lying half conscious on the floor in the assembly hall in Weston Secondary School. He didn't know whether this was the truth, but he had their full attention.

'Rose. His name was Rose-something.'

'Chief Inspector Rosewall,' said the voice, 'yes, sir.'

'Tell Rosewall. Tell him he's the one who took my brief-case. And get a car here.'

'There'll be a car with you in ten minutes.'

'Ten minutes is no bloody good,' George said. 'He'll be up and away by then.'

He went back and stood on the corner opposite the school gate, hopping up and down trying to keep his bad foot off the ground. He didn't know if Martin was still inside. He could have come out while George was in the phone box.

He ran his hand through his hair. His fingers were bloody. There was blood on the side of his face and the collar of his shirt.

It was starting to rain. The raindrops felt like ice on his face.

The police were probably less than ten minutes but it seemed like hours. George kept looking up and down the road and then back at the school and then up and down the road again. There was no traffic at all. There was nobody else in the street. If Martin came out now, he didn't know what he would do.

The police car came round the corner and George waved and hobbled towards it. As the car pulled up beside him and one of the policemen stuck his head out of the window, George saw Martin come staggering out of the school gate. He took one look at George and the police car and set off at a run.

'Mr Potter?' said the policeman.

'That's him,' George said, pointing at Martin, who was half-way to the corner of the street already. 'That's him. That's the one.'

'You'd better get in the car, Mr Potter.'

'That's him, for God's sake.'

The other policeman got out of the car and ran down the road. Martin had already disappeared round the corner.

Audrey opened the front door. She had heard them coming up the path. She was in her dressing-gown but she hadn't been to bed.

'Thank God,' she said. 'I've been going crazy.'

George was outside, soaking wet, with his head in bandages, and accompanied by two policemen.

'Tell him he's the one who had my briefcase,' he was saying. 'Tell Rosewall he's the one who stole it.'

'Yes,' said the policeman.

'And tell him to let me know as soon as you catch him, as soon as anything happens. Tell him to ring me here.'

'I'll tell him.'

Audrey thanked the policemen and shut the door and got George inside and sat him on the sofa. She helped him get his wet coat and his shoes off and turned the fire up. There was a bottle of whisky and a glass on the table.

'Are you on the bottle at this hour of the morning?' he said.

'I've been going crazy,' she said. She sat down in an armchair and poured herself a whisky. 'Do you want one?'

'I'd better not.'

'When you didn't come back, I kept ringing your place. You weren't there. The pubs were shut. I didn't know what had happened to you.'

'Quite a lot.'

'Tell,' she said.

George told. He told her about going to the school and about his fight with Martin and about the police arriving. She made him describe the whole thing twice, questioning him about the details.

'So there we were,' he said, 'driving round in the rain. One policeman on foot and me in the car with the other one. Going round and round the streets in the rain. No sign of him. They could have had him if they'd been a bit faster.'

'They'll find him,' she said. 'Don't worry.'

'And then the other car turns up and they tell me it'll take me to casualty and they'll go on looking. I didn't want to go. Not until they'd caught him. But they said they had cars out everywhere looking for him. They said I ought to go to casualty and get my head seen to.'

'Quite right,' she said. 'They'll find him.'

'I've got two stitches in here,' he said, tapping the side of his head. He lifted his foot up. 'And a bandage on here.'

'You've been in the wars all right,' she said. She poured herself another drink. 'Do you want to have a bath and get changed? Do you want to go to bed? You look awful.'

'No, I couldn't. I'll probably sleep all day tomorrow.' He was wide awake now. 'When I told them his name, they knew who he was. They already knew about him. I don't understand any of it. All right, he put the photos in the briefcase. I understand that. But why? And what was he doing in the school? Why did he attack me? I'd never heard of him until a few days ago.'

'I've been thinking about that,' she said. 'Do you want to talk about it?'

'Go on.'

'Suppose I was right all along. I said there was somebody close to you.'

'He isn't close to me.'

'No,' she said, 'I know, but suppose there was somebody else. Suppose there were two of them. Then it starts to make sense.'

'There wasn't anybody else there.'

'How do you know?' She had a gulp of her whisky. 'Look, you come staggering into the hall, crashing and banging and knocking chairs over. They're up in the balcony. You heard the seat bang. Now, if they're up in the balcony and you're down in the hall, how do they get out without being seen?'

'Through the door?' he said.

'Oh, George, think. You know the school better than I do. How do they get from the balcony to the door?'

'All right,' he said, 'they go out at the back of the balcony and come down the stairs.'

'When are they visible to somebody coming out of the hall?'

'About half-way down the stairs, I suppose. But there isn't any "they". There's just him.'

'How much light was there on the stairs?'

'Quite a bit. Better than in the hall.'

'Right,' she said. 'So, from the moment they're half-way down the stairs they're visible to anybody coming out of the hall. They didn't know who you were. They didn't know where you were except that you were in the hall. They didn't know you were up on the stage. They didn't know you were too pissed to put one foot in front of the other. You could have come through those doors at any moment. All you had to do was stick your head out. They couldn't risk it.'

'So?'

'So what do they do? One of them comes into the hall to find out who you are and what you're doing. And to make sure you stay where you are while the other one escapes. You heard a door shut, remember? The rest of it, well . . . you think he's threatening you, he thinks you're threatening him. What always happens with men in that situation? They start fighting.'

'But I saw him anyway.'

'Not him,' she said. 'It's the other one who matters. They have to assume you're somebody to do with the school. Otherwise, what are you doing there? You're probably a member of staff. You mustn't see them both. You mustn't even catch a glimpse of the other one because you'd recognize him. If you see him with the man who found your briefcase, you'll put two and two together.'

'I don't know,' he said. 'Anyway, that doesn't explain what they were doing there in the first place.'